D1736154

Savior

by
Martha Kennedy

As regards the uncertainty about everything...the city of God
thoroughly detests such doubt as madness.
(St. Augustine, *The City of God*)

Second Edition

Thanks to Beth Bruno for her expert assistance editing the
manuscript.
Thanks to Nile Johnson, Marcia Gieck and Ginger Sickbert for their
careful and enthusiastic reading of an early draft.

For my Grandmother Beall

Book One: Called

Chapter 1, Minnesingers

"...my heart was utterly darkened; and whatever I beheld was death. My native country was a torment to me, and my father's house a strange unhappiness... I fretted...sighed, wept, was distracted; had neither rest nor counsel. For I bore about a shattered and bleeding soul..." St. Augustine, *Confessions*

The signs of wet misery weighed as heavily as the rain. Of all the nearby roads, only the one leading up the hill to the castle was not flooded. Villagers scrambled to higher ground to find safety from the flooding river. They huddled on the roadway beside the castle walls in lean-tos made of hide and branches and warmed themselves over their smoking, sputtering cook fires.

Conrad and Rudolf, and their father Heinrich, were continually at the service of travelers, who, once their carts or wagons were pried loose, came into the hall to wait out the storm. Friars and tradesmen, noblemen and their vassals, knights and pilgrims, all trapped for who knew how long, sighed and agreed the river would continue to rise. Dogs straggled in, shook the water from their fur and curled up before the fire to sleep. No one had the heart to send them back into the rain. The fire behind Conrad sent the smells of wet wool, dogs, food, sweat, incense and damp straw into the room. Conrad thumped his fist on the bench, keeping time to the minnesinger and hating life.

Conrad's older brother, Rudolf, sat to one side of the fire, his fingers entwined with those of Gretchen, his fiancée. They looked at each other in calf-eyed adoration as the rain-stranded minnesinger sang one love song after another.

God made her cheeks a true delight
In which his richest color glows
The deepest red, the purest white
Here, like a lily, there a rose
I hope it's not a sin to say
I'd rather watch her blushes than
Admire the starry Milky Way
But why should I, oh foolish man
Place her so high above me?
My praise would cause me pain,
Were she too proud to love me.

As far as Conrad could see, there was nothing "...like a lily, there a rose" in the girl who sat beside Rudolf. She was completely ordinary, yet his brother had given over his life to her in oaths of undying faith and sentimental devotion. And, thought Conrad, even if Gretchen were such a woman as this singer sang about, what had his brother done to win her? Conrad was certain there had been no great deeds of valor to raise his morose and silent brother above all other men and to make this silly looking girl love him, nothing more noble than shoveling manure from the stable of Sir Adelbert.

Conrad ached to be sent away to train under a knight, to serve and learn the rules of chivalry. He wanted to take leave from this house, his father, the horses, but his father insisted, "There is no need to send you outside. All you need to learn you can learn here. Your job will be the horses, their care, their breeding." Conrad hated the idea that he was destined to be his brother's servant! He would make the better knight, the better Lord of Lunkhofen!

Conrad loved the travelers' stories of faraway cities, strange animals in distant countries, crusading knights and wild, brave battles. But he was here instead, thumping on the bench, as though its simple rough surface would give way to the larger world.

"Something else, minnesinger!" called a man from across the hall. "Such songs are well and good for the son of our host here and his bride, but for the rest of us? Sing of adventure, or tell us a story. The rainy days are long enough without this endless harping on love. Sing of heroes!"

The minnesinger turned to Rudolf, who nodded. "Forgive me, young sir. Perhaps bad luck in love has left them bitter." Others in the hall laughed at the man who'd cried out, but no one objected when the minnesinger struck a melancholy, aching chord on his guitar. He sang alone.

> *Alas, all my years, where have they disappeared?*
> *Have I dreamed my life, or is it real?*
> *That which I thought was something, was it something?*
> *Perhaps I have been sleeping, and do not know it.*
> *Now I am awake and all seems strange*
> *That used to be familiar, once, as my own hand*
> *The people and the place where I grew up*
> *Seem alien, like lies, not of my own land.*

To Conrad the song was just the bitter railing of old men. "*In my day,*" they all began; even his father said, "*When I was a young man like you…*" Conrad thought the changes were mostly in themselves. Their youth flown, they saw the world as having grown worse.

"*Alas, how miserable are the young today,*" the minnesinger sang while those around nodded in agreement. "*Who runs after pleasures here, has lost them there, ever more, alas.*"

"Stupid," thought Conrad. "As bad as the weather." He pounded his fist on the bench, this time hard enough that he pulled it back in pain. If the rain would stop, he could at least ride.

Rudolf was lost in thought. Their father felt uneasy, knowing well where the song was going.

The other musicians began to accompany the minnesinger

9

when the song changed from solitary reverie. The bagpipe and reed pipe followed the lyrics to the song's questioning conclusion.

Alas, how the sweet things poison us
I see the bitter gall floating in the honey
The white green red world is beautiful outside,
And inside black, as dark as death.
Whomever it has seduced, let him look where he will find
comfort.
With a soft penance, he is set free from mighty sin.
Knights, think of this, it is for you, these words,
You wear the bright helms, the hard rings,
The strong shields, the consecrated swords.
Would God that I myself were worthy of the victory.
I, a needy man, would win great wages
Yet not acres of land or the gold of kings
I myself would wear the crown of ages
That any soldier fighting for his money can win with his
spear
If I could make that beloved voyage across the sea
I would sing "Joy!" and never more "Alas,"
Never more, "Alas."

When the song began – a song familiar to all – Rudolf looked away from Gretchen, though he kept his fingers twined in hers. Was this, Gretchen's small hand and their life together, the happiness for which he should strive? That the pleasure he felt at her touch was more than he had expected made Rudolf uneasy. Gray foreboding crept into the space opened by doubt and told him that nothing so wonderful could last.

Rudolf was not Conrad. He was close to his mother, who, in her moments of despair and loneliness, had read to him from the *Lives of the Saints*, one of the two books she owned. With its leather covers, bronze hinges and small lock, it was a precious thing kept wrapped in an embroidered and quilted linen cover. "There is no hardship that we cannot bear if we are as brave as the saints. It is God's will that in this life we have little pleasure and much suffering."

Rudolf found his joy in Gretchen troubling. He had once mentioned this to his father who replied that man was worthless unless he brought children into the world. "What else could be God's work?" he had said. "You and your Gretchen will fill Schneebeli's big house, your home, with children. You need not worry about anything save nature, and it does no good to worry over that. Nature will as she will."

At the end of the song, the hall applauded and called for more of the same, and so the minnesinger chose a song to satisfy his fatigued and rain-trapped audience, a song that carried Heinrich's sons toward a decision that would break their parents' hearts.

Now my life has gained some meaning
Since these sinful eyes behold
The sacred land with meadows greening
Whose renown is often told.
This was granted me from God:
To see the land, the holy sod,
Which in human form He trod...
Christians, Jews, Muslims contending,
Claim it as a legacy
May God judge with grace unending
Through His blessed Trinity.
Strife is heard on every hand:
Ours the only just demand,
He will have us rule the land.

In the wailing pipes, Conrad heard adventure, faraway places, danger and a hero's death, not, of course that *he* would die.

In the drum beats Rudolf heard the call of service in the glory of Christ, of salvation. When the song was finished, Heinrich called the minnesinger aside.

"Is the Holy Father calling for a crusade?"

"My lord, you know a crusade against the unfaithful is always the wish of the Holy Father. That does not change."

"What of the Emperor's treaty?"

"It was for ten years and that time has passed."

"And you would fight?"

"Were I wealthy enough to outfit myself, young enough to do some good. But," he sighed, "this will not be my fight, though in my heart it is my fight. In my young days, I went. Twice."

"You never married."

"No, my lord."

Heinrich looked quickly at his wife who was looking intently at Rudolf. Anna wanted this marriage; she wanted grandchildren, and she knew her son as no one else did. This was not music she wanted him to hear. She knew of Conrad's restlessness. It was unlikely they could stop him if he chose to go, but Rudolf worried her, sitting quietly with his Gretchen, his eyes cast down.

Gretchen was pale and looked at her beloved in bewilderment. In a very few minutes she had gone from the center of his gaze to the edges of his world. She knew it, but she knew not why. She anxiously searched her memory for some ill-chosen word she might have spoken to cause Rudolf to retreat.

***

"I left my wife," Heinrich motioned with his head toward Anna. "For years she was alone. Rudolf was nearly a man when I returned. Conrad did not know me at all."

"This was her sacrifice to God. Surely you think of it that way."

"She was in danger, our home was in danger, constantly. You know as well as I that in our lives there has never been peace. If no one makes war on us, we fight each other."

The minnesinger nodded. "It is a great waste that it is so."

Heinrich looked toward a slit window high above. For him, war had lost its glory long ago. He had been in Egypt in time for the opening of Damietta. After months of besieging the city, the Crusaders found a guard tower abandoned. Heinrich rushed in with others, joyous in victory. Their short-lived triumph found nothing more than empty, burned-out buildings lining sad, narrow streets filled with the bloated bodies of men, women and children who had starved to death, food for dogs. From there, he had known hunger and desperate thirst. He witnessed the near massacre of the foot soldiers, men who had gone with him from the towns in his fief, men he had known as boys. And when it was over, the city they had fought so hard to retain was turned over to the Egyptian sultan, al-Kamil.

The Crusaders believed that these losses had befallen them because they were not led by God's knight, but by a Cardinal who knew nothing of war strategy. Bitter and defeated, they returned to the ships the Egyptians had seized, held and returned to them. Weary, they turned toward home. The first part of the journey had been easy, but once they arrived on Lombard soil, travel became slow and dangerous, threading their way between the armies of the Pope and those of the Emperor. Many were captured or killed on the way.

***

When Heinrich again walked up the hill to his castle gate, he had been gone nearly ten years. His oldest was ready to begin the journey into knighthood, and his second son ran wild in the forest making mock war on everything. Heinrich returned with two Arabian mares and the determination to remain at home, to breed horses and to raise his children. That the Pope's army had returned with the True Cross meant nothing to Heinrich.

"Gold is quickly gone," Heinrich had told his boys. "These lovely mares will be like the goose that laid the golden egg. More gold will come from them." He was right. He became well known for his horses, and though many knights were slowly reduced in their lives to an existence little better than that of their tenants and peasants, Heinrich prospered. "All we need to do, my sons, is remain at peace and live our lives."

***

Conrad was looking into the fire. "I could go," he thought, "just to get away from this." The minnesinger sang of a destiny beyond raising horses for other men to ride. "What is there here for me beyond servitude to my brother and this trafficking in horses? There is the church." He winced, jabbing at the fire with the long poker that rested against the wall, making the sparks fly, brilliant, short-lived red stars against the tiny firmament of soot-stained stone, and outside it continued to rain. Though no one moved in the hall, everything central to the family had changed.

***

"To fight for God, to take up the Cross and fight, is that not glory?"

"Not glory." Heinrich brushed the shoulder of the four-year-old chestnut mare standing between him and his son. Conrad brushed the opposite flank. "Nightmare. Many – most – never even make it. In my time, thousands died in Sicily on board ship. Boats of death, they turned back to save the lives of the few who had survived. And for those who make it to the Holy Land? There is death on the road. There is death in battle. There is death on the return."

Conrad thought that even if he died, he would have seen something. It was salvation enough to leave this hilltop, to go beyond the two villages that made up his father's fief, to see beyond the mountains all around him, the places he knew. "Salvation, Father, is not nothing. Even if I die on the way, I would have salvation."

Heinrich smiled. He was sure that his boy was not much interested in the afterlife, not this child of the here and now.

The thoughts Heinrich did not speak would be heard by most as sacrilege, such sacrilege as was common to hungry and thirsty men crossing the desert where men either lose God or see God. In the desert mountains lived wild solitary men who talked constantly to God in the dark seclusion of their caves. Heinrich knew Conrad could endure the physical hardship and would not be much troubled by the spiritual struggle. He was young enough to be molded, to submit if he believed his submission would take him where he wanted to go. He would be happy in the discipline of the knightly priest. None of this knowledge made Heinrich like what his son was bent on. "Truth is, the minnesinger put a bug in your ear."

"What am I supposed to do? Stay here? For what?" The truth burst from Conrad, and he attempted to cover it. "I would serve God, Father."

"You can read and write. If you are so eager to serve God, go into the church and stay here."

"I want to serve God with my sword, Father. To regain the Holy City in His name."

Heinrich laughed. "Conrad," he said, "it is natural at your age to want adventure."

Conrad scowled. "Father, it seems a man would want to make his own way."

"Then make your way HERE. We all must make our way in any case, regardless of what is left us by our fathers; our destiny depends on the wheel of fate. We have very little to say about that. It is God's will and that is always God's business."

"But you went."

"I was forced."

"Forced?"

"I had no choice. Our land comes with the price of life; that is the risk, and of course we pay our duty, more every year as these wars continue."

"If they come I will go, Father."

"In that case, you and your brother will go, unless, please God, they decide to spare the oldest son. To lose you both would break your mother's heart. Finish up, son," said Heinrich and left shaking his head. He could force Conrad to remain, but what good would that do?

Sheltered from the rain by the row of lindens growing opposite the outer wall, Heinrich walked slowly around the castle, his head bowed, his hands clasped behind his back. In his childhood, it had been but one tower, the keep, two walls. The old walls remained, but his father, on his return from the Holy Land, had built up the back wall and installed an oven and a large kitchen and stables of half-timber filled with rubble and rock. Castle Lunkhofen was half fort/half home. His grandfather, the first Heinrich, had, in his time, replaced the wood and earthwork castle with the stone tower and walls, a lesson brought home by crusading knights and applied directly to their own castles to improve their safety.

His family had seen three generations of crusading knights, and his own young son would have it be a fourth. Would he return to add something to the castle? There was no way to know.

***

Heinrich searched the sky. The rain had slowed, certainly. People were gathering their belongings to continue their journeys. The minnesinger, sensing that he and his troupe had outworn their welcome, left the following morning after a conversation with Rudolf that went well into the night.

"The situation is grave, my young lord. The infidels again have Jerusalem. The Emperor's treaty has expired and everything is now in a state of confusion. It does not help that the Emperor himself has been excommunicated and every venture made on his behalf is condemned by the Holy Father." Many of the minnesinger's songs had been about German gold draining into the coffers of the Italian Pope who had anathematized the Emperor.

Rudolf was thoughtful, then asked, "How is it to fight for God so far away?"

"Unforgettable. It is difficult to say to one who has not seen it. There are great heroes; battle is glorious."

"But what of salvation?"

"Yes. Each man finds salvation. Here, on the brink of your bright future with your beloved, you cannot know how human life is filled with doubt. Our purpose is not clear; the snares of human life abound and we cannot see well enough to keep ourselves free. None of us has strength enough to escape Satan's traps, and so the divine promise is out of reach. Everlasting life, young lord. I have gone twice, and all my sins count as nothing. This is an immense relief."

Rudolf could imagine it would be. Rudolf's mind held all the torments of Hell, the endless dark and the overhanging, blackened branches of a dead world. He knew the fires; they pursued his thoughts every moment. In these intervals of his life, nothing could give him pleasure or ease. He went to his bed at night tormented and afraid and awoke with a jolt soon after drifting into sleep. If he slept through to morning, it was to awaken with a sense of dread that dropped quickly into despair. He confessed the wish to kill himself, and was given hard penance to counteract the desire to commit this most horrible of sins, but fasting and prayer failed to win for him his freedom. Then the darkness passed, and the earth regained its beauty. He rose then from the bottomless void where he had been living and again walked easily on the surface of God's earth with other men.

During the lonely, often frightening times when her husband was gone on Crusade, Anna had held the little boy to her and together they had prayed for Heinrich to return, for the castle to remain safe. Anna was barely fourteen when she married. Her own father had died years before, and Heinrich became her husband and her father. The little boy felt his mother's fear in his young heart, and his serious mind searched anxiously within its small compass of experience for a solution to her problem. He could only stay by her. Her sorrow and loneliness took permanent hold within him; Anna became – though she would have been very sad to know it – a shadow in his soul. He felt that he must be a husband in his father's stead, a burden too large for a boy. In this he had been – of course – unable to succeed. No matter what he did, her misery remained. He could not fill the spot belonging to his father, and so he grew into manhood convinced that he was not enough.

He had felt peaceful and happy with Gretchen. She was simple and straightforward, young, and truly kind. She laughed easily and playfully. Gretchen saw in Rudolf a man he had not known himself to be, and he found a way to love himself. But the minnesinger had broken Rudolf's peace. Rudolf felt himself withdraw from the gentle girl as the web of black threads began weaving itself around his mind. All his prayers led him to the same place; if he went on Crusade, he would return free forever of the great fear of Hell in which he lived.

"Have you ever felt," began Rudolf tentatively, "have you ever felt such an emptiness inside that you…" he stopped. Had he said too much?

"Doubted God?" said the minnesinger.

Rudolf looked down and away.

"All men have these moments, my young lord. It is the tempter."

A cold pit of fear opened in Rudolf's breast. So he had been right. Satan was reaching for him. If the sweet things he had found with Gretchen were evil and the darkness he had known before was evil, what of him was not evil? All was evil. His heart pounded in a sudden surge of desperate fear. *I am doomed*, he thought. *There is no way out for me*. If the shadow inside of him could be removed once and for all by fighting for Jerusalem, he would go. His future would be filled with light and he would be free.

***

The rain finally stopped; the hall emptied of visitors and was thoroughly scrubbed for spring, clean rush matting spread upon the stone floors. The normal routine of summer life absorbed everyone. Gretchen returned home to help her mother and sisters prepare her trousseau, for the wedding would take place just after harvest. Grass and grain grew tall in the fields. The brothers' days were long and when night came, Rudolf and Conrad collapsed, exhausted. Conrad's claustrophobic restlessness faded a bit in the outdoor work, but for Rudolf there was no peace, not even in exhaustion. In the consuming chores of summer Heinrich tried to hold on to the belief that the minnesinger's words had stirred nothing within his sons.

Chapter 2, The Black Horse

On the day of the late summer fair in Zürich, men and horses left the castle in darkness to reach the city before dawn, threading their way down the mountain to the shining Zürichsee. To one side of the market square were several long wooden bars resting on posts set in the ground. It was here that Heinrich, Conrad and Heinrich's groom tied the horses – mostly mares and foals – they hoped to sell that day. At intervals along this bar were carved stone troughs, which each horse's owner filled from the well. Conrad and his father worked quickly to get straw under the horses' hooves; the foals were not shod, their feet having known only the soft grass and soil of the pasture and the dirt and straw of the stable. Most of Heinrich's mares were not for sale but had been brought along to show the stock from which the young horses came. Heinrich's horses were beautiful and expensive, known as exemplary riding animals.

For two years, Conrad had been training a black colt, a young warhorse. The horse would be sold, along with other horses. Early in the summer, he had secretly ridden the colt at a tournament, and boy and horse had come out winners.

Heinrich's shield, horizontal stripes, alternating blue and white representing mountains and rivers, crossed by a red pole, top to bottom, hung above the shining mares and colts, telling all who passed that these were the horses of Heinrich von Lunkhofen. He hoped to make enough for Rudolf's wedding and to set up the young man's household, expecting the two-year-old destrier Conrad had trained would go for a good price.

Conrad leaned on the bar with one hand absently stroking the nose of his colt and looked down the wide thoroughfare that led to the square in the center of town. At the top of the square was the well.

Farmers brought fruit, vegetables, cheeses and sausages and negotiated in muffled voices with traveling tradesmen for a space in the square. Some had carts they cleverly transformed into a seller's stall. Others carried their shops on their backs, folding tables and shelves. This small world of commerce gave the people a chance to see many exotic items from the East; silks dyed in fantastic colors, brassware, glass from Venice.

Against the wall of the town hall was a permanent, elevated stage. It was a piece of a wider world, reflecting in its time all sides of public culture -- acrobats, public chastisements, the execution of justice, Christmas pageants, mystery plays, sermons, and music.

From where he stood, Conrad could see most of the market. He had chosen that particular spot, knowing his day could be long. Buyers would come and go, bargain and tarry, and much of success lay in calm waiting. The stage was directly in front of him, some 30 yards distant. Though he could not wander around the fair, he could at least, from here, watch the stage.

"Heinrich! Beautiful horses!"

"Ah, Mülner. Yes, we've had a good year," said Heinrich, greeting the Mayor.

"When's the wedding?"

"Just after harvest."

"So soon!"

Heinrich looked past Mülner into the town and back toward the road leading from the north. Potential buyers had let him know they would come early to see the best he had. He was anxious. He would be happy to have the business done. "You're invited, of course, you and your wife."

"And what of this young man? Have you a bride in mind?" The Mayor had three daughters.

"He's young. His mind is still on tournaments and horses. I don't think he has thought of love." Heinrich reached for his younger son's head and tousled his hair it as if he were a child. Conrad ducked and dodged his father's hand, but he grinned. He was nearly his father's size. "You see? He doesn't know if he's boy or man."

"I'm a man, Father," said Conrad.

"Ha, there you are, Heinrich, the child has spoken!"

Conrad glowered.

Heinrich sighed. "Someday, son, you will understand why I would slow time if I could."

"We missed a great deal, did we not, Heinrich?"

"We did. Rudolf was a child when I left. He'd grown nearly to manhood when I returned. Well, we returned, and that, old friend, is the important thing."

Conrad kicked at the straw in disgust. Whenever these two met it was the same conversation, the wasted years and how wonderful it was to be home. Conrad hoped to hear of their adventures, but it was always this instead.

"They are preaching a new Crusade."

"Ah no. And where this time? The Holy Land or the unholy lands to the east?"

"Palestine. Last night they dined with me. They are following the markets on the Pope's business."

Conrad's heart beat wildly. Heinrich looked quickly at his son, but Conrad had turned to look at the shining colt. "They are a pair," thought Heinrich, "well-trained, compliant, amiable, but inside?" He had watched his son train this young horse to ride under an armored man with a lance; it was with joy the colt accepted the burden of a rider and rapture that led him toward the post and hoop at which Conrad charged.

"Where is the young lord?"

"He is bringing his mother."

"I will stop by later, then." The mayor bowed at Heinrich and nodded to Conrad whose heart still beat in a way he wished it would not. He felt almost as if his father could see through the skin and bones of his chest.

"Well, son," said Heinrich, "it looks as if we will learn something today."

Conrad was silent. He would not speak of his hopes to his father, not at that moment.

"For now, we'll tend to business. The future shows itself with no effort from us. Hand me that pail." He gestured at a wooden bucket filled with oats. "I'll feed the mares. You see that they are watered."

Grateful for an occupation, Conrad took two pitch-lined pails to the well. An elegantly dressed man caught up to him and tapped his shoulder, "Young Lunkhofen, tell me about that black colt. Your father said you know more than he." Conrad turned to see Duke von Schnabelberg, his father's lord.

"He has an easy seat, swift and smooth, my lord."

"It is you who trained him, not your father?"

"Since he was four months old."

"How is he at a tilt?"

"Straight. Very swift, my lord."

"Have you run him at an opponent or only at a tilting pole?"

"I ran him at a tournament last month at the fair here, in Zürich."

"Have you not heard? The Holy Father in Rome has again banned tournaments."

The two walked back to the horses. Heinrich winked at his son and took the buckets from him.

"Can I give him a go-over?" von Schnabelberg asked, turning to Heinrich.

"Certainly, my lord, feel free," said Heinrich. The horse stood above sixteen hands, but for all his power and size, he was very gentle. Duke von Schnabelberg pulled back the horse's lips to look at his teeth, felt his flanks to check the musculature, and ran his hand down the forelegs to get a sense of the density of his bones. He lifted a foot to check the hoof. Conrad fed the young stallion apple slices, and the horse bore everything philosophically.

The man turned to Heinrich and said, "A fine horse. He might be what I'm looking for. I would ride him."

"Do so, my lord Duke. Conrad here will go with you."

"I'll leave my horse here as security." The duke put the reins of the dun palfrey in Heinrich's hands, and he and Conrad walked the black colt to the tournament field. When they reached a clear, grassy space, they stopped. Conrad handed the duke the reins, then threaded his fingers together, and leaned down to give the man a hand-up.

"How are the stirrups, my lord?"

"A bit short. You need to stand more forward on a horse like this to reach the enemy with a sword."

Conrad set the stirrups down two notches. "Does that suit you, my lord?"

"It will do." Von Schnabelberg sighed. "A man who wants to buy horses should bring his own tack."

The saddle on which he sat was new; it had been made for this horse and would go with the horse when it was sold. Conrad fumed at the man's remark and considered the cost of the saddle. The duke put spurs to horse and the colt leapt forward. Conrad felt an unexpected pang as he watched them in flight away from him. This duke could come and go as he pleased. There was but one use for a horse such as this with tournaments forbidden. He imagined the horse seeing worlds he would never see and his soul burned. "I raised and trained him for that freedom," he fumed, "and I am my father's slave." He hit his fist against his leg, and winced. "Ah, well, if the Mayor spoke true, then how can my father stop me?"

Von Schnabelberg roused the colt to a full run. He stood forward on the saddle, sword upraised, as if he were charging an enemy. The black colt seemed to respond in joy to the man's mastery, and Conrad felt the mysterious pang again. What if the duke bought the horse? Would there ever be another like him? Conrad's thoughts wandered to the comments of the Mayor, and he was eager to get back inside to see if the priests would preach a crusade as he desperately hoped. It would give him an argument to use with his father. His youth was against him, but he did not want to wait until he was older. What if everything ended, and he had no chance — his one opportunity lost?

Conrad was startled when the duke rode up beside him.

"Help me dismount. Tell me all you can about the horse."

"You've ridden him, my lord. He has told you everything." Conrad's voice carried an edge of bitterness. He looked at the ground as he walked.

"Has he been ridden much?"

"I ride him daily."

"By others?"

"My father, my brother Rudolf, but yes, mostly I have ridden him. He has been mine to train. My father has ridden him mostly to check the horse's progress."

"I see. He has been your horse since he was born."

Conrad felt the strange pang again. What was this?

"Do we talk prices, or do I talk with your father?"

"My father."

Von Schnabelberg may have held the reins, but the war horse ambled sweetly behind Conrad, from time to time bumping the back of Conrad's head with his nose.

"Well, my lord?" asked Heinrich, meeting them halfway. From this Conrad knew Rudolf and their mother had arrived. Heinrich had left Rudolf with the groom and the horses, coming out himself to talk business with the duke.

"He's a wonderful mount, no question. You breed beautiful horses. What are you asking for Conrad here? Does he come with the stallion?"

Heinrich laughed. "If I sold you my son, I would have no one to train horses such as that one!" He nodded toward the stallion and named a price.

"That's too much, unless this boy *does* come with it!"

"My lord duke, you know you will not find such a charger anywhere else."

"That may be true, but I have the leisure and the money to look."

"You would have more leisure if you saved yourself the trouble of looking further!" Heinrich chided his customer.

In the end, Heinrich asked more than Duke von Schnabelberg wanted to pay, and Heinrich would not drop the price. Though others looked at the young stallion, the black horse stayed.

Chapter 3, The Black Robes

Mendicant friars were a familiar sight. They often came through the towns preaching and begging alms. The Pope had found them useful organs for promoting Papal interests among the people. They wandered throughout Europe selling indulgences and preaching Crusades – itself an indulgence for which one risked his life. Christ had given his life in exchange for mankind's horrendous sins; that a man would fight in his turn for the Cross seemed not much to ask. Conrad stood beside his brother. Their attention was fixed on the black-robed men standing to one side of the stage.

"When they speak, we won't be able to hear them," said Conrad.

"All the better," replied Heinrich bitterly. Anna nodded.

"I will go down closer to listen," said Conrad, restless.

Heinrich could not argue. He expected no customers when the friars were speaking; the mysterious promise of religion would hold them fast until the friar's message had been delivered. "Come back here the moment the black robes are finished. There are buyers who will come for those two black geldings, the bay mare and her foal, and the chestnut palfrey stallion. I will need your help."

Conrad grabbed his brother's sleeve and pulled him along. His mother, making the same gesture, pulled Rudolf toward her. Torn between the two, Rudolf stood bewildered for a moment, then he gently removed his mother's fingers from his sleeve and went on with his brother. Anna looked up at him. Then she looked at Heinrich, who shrugged. He could not stop them; they were men. Anna clenched her hands into small fists and turned away.

The press of the crowd made it impossible for Rudolf and Conrad to get near, but both were tall enough to see. The acrobats had cleared away their gear, and the stage lay empty. The crowd waited expectantly, coughing, clearing throats, murmuring, shuffling their feet, eyes mostly forward, talking amongst themselves. A trio of musicians and a minnesinger stepped on stage first. One beat a brightly ribboned tambour and danced back and forth across the front, attracting attention. The third held a horn. The fourth readied a bagpipe made of goatskin. The song began with the horn sounding across the square like Gabriel's trumpet, then the pipe joined in before the minnesinger struck a chord on his lute, and began:

> *Now my life has gained some meaning*
> *Since these sinful eyes behold*
> *The sacred land with meadows greening*
> *Whose renown is often told.*
> *This was granted me from God:*
> *To see the land, the holy sod*
> *Which in human form He trod...*

Hearing this song, Rudolf felt the skin on his arms rise in chilled bumps, and he could see his destiny stretch out in front of him. "It's true then," he whispered.

"Wait. We will soon know."

The song finished. The musicians moved to the back as the Dominican friars took the stage.

One held a silver cross high in front of him. Everyone spoke in one voice, "*In nomine Patris, et Filii, et Spiritus Sancti.*" It was enough to silence the crowd. The other, Brother Friedrich, was to speak. He was a master at this. He traveled the entire German-speaking world recruiting men to the Cross. He stepped forward and led the crowd in prayer, in German. "Our Heavenly Father, bless the assembly. Bless and aid the Holy Father, Innocente IV, in Rome, who is beset with concerns over the governance of your holy kingdom here on earth. Bless our illustrious Emperor, Frederick the Second, who has striven to keep peace in your sacred country these past ten years. Please, Heavenly Father, heal the rift between our

Holy Father and our Emperor. Give us the courage to continue the battle against the enemies of Christ wherever we may find them. Guide us that we are not so concerned with the welfare of our flesh that we neglect to provide for the welfare of our souls. Teach us to follow thy will, for our earthly lives are fleeting and our hope is Heaven. We ask these blessings *in nomine Patris, et Filii, et Spiritus Sancti*, Amen." He stood a few moments in dramatic silence.

Then, in a clear voice, he said, "Are you sure of Heaven? Will you sit beside our Holy Savior for all eternity? Have you no sins to your account? Are you sure that Satan has no hold on you?"

The crowd was hushed, each heart afraid.

Ten yards distant, a knife grinder sat behind an amazing machine, a carved wooden statue of the devil. The statue's face was painted red and its horns were black. Above a sneering grin, black and white eyes bulged from his face. When the knife sharpener worked the foot pedal to spin the stone, the Devil's eyes spun, and his pointed tongue went in and out of his mouth. The grinding of the whetstone against metal made him appear to snarl and growl. The crowd turned to this figure all at the same moment, embarrassing the poor knife sharpener, who was trying to catch up on the backlog of work while the Dominicans held everyone's attention.

"In the hands of Satan you will suffer unending pain. You will be the knife on that grinder's wheel, turning forever and ever, eternally separated from our Holy Father, the worst suffering of all."

People in the crowd were afraid. All day they had enjoyed the beautiful things they seldom saw, the music and acrobats, jugglers and mimes on the stage, the opportunity to trade what they no longer needed for something they did. They imagined the comfort new goods would bring to their lives and took pride in their wealth. Men ogled the women who passed and imagined how this or that would be better than their wife at home. "What I wouldn't do with that! If only!" Another held a hot grilled sausage between two pieces of thick bread in his fat hand, one of a dozen he had eaten that day.

"Look around," said the priest. "It's easy for us to see the sins of others. It is not so easy to see our own sins, but our Heavenly

Father sees what we can -- or will -- not. He sees even our hidden sins. Remember, 'All come short of the glory of God.' Are you not afraid?" The priest understood the narrow line between faith and superstition; he knew these people.

Rudolf was white with fear. The sins of others, yes. He saw this man's gluttony and that man's lechery; he had known liars and knew well there were murderers and brigands. It was for this his father's castle was fortified, and the people of the village rushed to it for safety. He could see THEIR sins, but what of his own?

"Would you have your sins forever cleaned away and the Kingdom of Heaven vouchsafed to you? Would you join our Holy Savior in the fight to save the world from sin?"

Who would not? Conrad looked around him at the crowd, waiting to hear more.

"How can you do this? How can your uncountable sins count as nothing? How can you help our Holy Savior? Those who believe in the Holy Church are His apostles. In the gospel of St. Matthew, Christ told his apostles, 'Think not that I am come to send peace on earth: I came not to send peace, but a sword.' We are charged by Christ to fight for his kingdom, to raise our swords and lances against all who are His enemies."

"And if you think, 'My wife will be alone' or 'My father and mother will be without their son,' remember Christ's words to his apostles, 'I am come to set man…against his father…a man's foes shall be they of his own household. He that loveth father or mother more than me is not worthy of me'."

"And if you think, 'I could die,' remember each man dies. It is lack of faith that makes us fear death, for Christ has said, "He that findeth his life shall lose it: and he that loseth his life for my sake shall find it.' He speaks of life everlasting with Him and Our Heavenly Father.

"It is the lot of man to die. Without the divine help of our Lord Jesus Christ we would have no hope of Heaven, no hope of redemption from our sins. Death of the flesh will come; death of the soul need never come, for as our Lord said, '…fear not they who kill the body, but are not able to kill the soul: but rather fear him who is able to destroy both soul and body in Hell.' It is yourselves you should fear. The tempter is with us at each moment, lulling us, stealing our courage, distracting us, leaving us heedless and complacent that he can influence our choices, offering us a path that seems easy but one that leads to our destruction. Mankind is weak; without the aid of our Lord Jesus Christ and his Blessed Mother we all would perish in Hell."

"What does Christ ask of us that we can be worthy of His love? He asks of us only what is for our own good; He tells His apostles, 'He that taketh not his cross and followeth after me is not worthy of me'. The love of our Holy Savior is perfect; He gave his life that we might live forever with Him in Heaven. Can we not do as much for Him? And for this we need fear no longer the consequences of our sinful nature."

"How, Father?" asked a man in the crowd who, thinking of his sins, had begun weeping. Many others had fallen to their knees in desperate fear. Everyone knew the Day of Judgment could come at any time. Maybe this was that day.

"How? You must give up everything, leave everything, all that is familiar, without wavering, knowing Christ has done as much for you. Even as I speak to you, the places made Holy by our Lord's life have fallen into the hands of those who deny the One True God. Our Holy Father in Rome, hearing of events in the Holy Land, has renewed his call for a crusade. Jerusalem is again in the hands of the infidel who, at the expiration of the agreement made with our Holy Roman Emperor, wasted no time in desecrating the holy sites and persecuting Christians living within its walls. Christian pilgrims are no longer safe on the long and difficult road leading to Jerusalem."

The crowd expressed outrage – how many of them had fought in the Holy Land? There were two generations of men standing there who had made this journey or the other to the pagan lands to the east. Many had worn the black cross of the Teutonic Knight on their shoulder; others the brown cape and white cross of the Knights Hospitaller.

"Must we fight forever?" asked a man in the crowd.

"The Holy Father himself has asked this question. As long as the infidel holds the true faith hostage, we must fight. Until the Holy City is forever in the control of the true believers, no Christian pilgrim will be safe. The Holy Father in Rome knows the dangers you will face on your journey and how natural it is for you, being men, to fear, but remember, it is only your earthly life you risk. He has sent me with this."

His companion gave him a roll of parchment. The audience could see that there was a great deal of writing and wondered if the friar would read all of it, but he rolled it to a place he had marked and began; "*We, therefore, trusting in the mercy of almighty God and in the authority of the blessed apostles, Peter and Paul, do grant, by the power of binding and loosing that God has conferred upon us, albeit unworthy, unto all those who undertake this work in person and at their own expense, full pardon for their sins about which they are heartily contrite and have spoken in confession...this general synod imparts the benefit of its blessings to all who piously set out on this common enterprise in order that it may contribute worthily to their salvation'.*"

"You will have full pardon for your sins. *Full* pardon for the sins you confess and for which you are truly contrite. For this? Do for Christ what Christ did for you. Take up the Cross and fight for the salvation of the Holy City."

"I know that some of you are too old to go; others have gone before and cannot go again. The Holy Father has thought of you, also, as you have heard, and for the help you give those who do go, your sins will also be forgiven."

Rudolf was shaking. This was God's message, then, the one for which he had prayed. There was this chance for him. The reward? Salvation, but only for sins he confessed. What of the sins he did not know? His stomach churned; he felt suddenly lightheaded. All was hopeless. Even this sacrifice might not save him.

"Conrad," he said hoarsely.

Conrad looked at Rudolf and saw the pallor of his face.

Something was wrong. A window had opened for him into Rudolf's guarded thoughts. "Rudolf, you are unwell."

"No, no, I am all right. Conrad, I must go now to this priest and take the vow."

"You cannot! You are to be married in two months time. You cannot marry after you take this vow. Marry first; then, if there is need, go."

"You do not understand, Conrad. It is not what I want to do; it is what I must do or there is no point for me to marry."

"Sssh!" said someone nearby. "I cannot hear."

Conrad scowled at the man; his brother's concerns were more pressing than anything these priests had to say.

"The situation is urgent. Our Holy Father in Rome has sent us to you," said the black robe. "If your heart tells you that this is the moment for you to take up the Cross for Our Lord, come to us, and we will talk to you, confess you if that is your need. We will be here the rest of the day. *Gloria Patri, et Filio, et Spiritui Sancto. Sicut erat in principio, et nunc, et semper, et in saecula saeculorum.* Amen."

The musicians stepped forward; the song they began was less rousing, more serious. A serious charge had been leveled on the audience, no question, and the song they sang concluded with an even stronger challenge:

> *They seek to escape from death and pain*
> *Who take no part in God's crusade,*
> *But this I know: their hope is vain*
> *And they have but themselves betrayed*
> *Who took the cross and gave no aid*
> *Will find in death his error plain*
> *And stand before the gate, dismayed*
> *Which opens wide for God's true thane.*

Anna wrung her hands. From the moment she had first seen Heinrich, she had loved him and clung to him with the ferocity of a child clinging to its mother. His concerns became hers; the castle became her home; his children became her world. On her wedding day she imagined she would be safe from more of the losses that had attended her life until then. She was mistaken. Loss of love is not the bad luck of childhood; it is the way of life. Her first child died within hours of birth, as did her second. She mourned each as if she had herself killed them and turned to the Holy Virgin for comfort and help. The bottom to Anna's faith was the loss of those who belonged to her; she could not consign them to God's care completely.

"At it again," Heinrich said, splitting the silence between them.

"They are always 'at it', as you say. It's enough to have Conrad riding at death in tournaments. He thinks he is immortal."

"I may not be able to hold him back, Anna, but I will do all that is in my power."

"He is like you."

Heinrich was in no mood to be baited again into this discussion. Anna would do this just to relieve some of her anxiety over her boys.

"Conrad is enough, too much, but Rudolf will go too."

"Rudolf? Why would Rudolf go? He is to be married."

"That will not stop him."

Rudolf was a mystery to Heinrich, whose intelligence was one of forthright common sense, pragmatism, and survival. He was a man of the open air and field. The music of the minnesingers, the beauty of tapestry, Anna's small treasure-trove of books, all the works of art and culture with which he filled his castle, were pursuits for idle moments, for others, for Anna. Anna could read and write; Heinrich had never needed these arts, and his mother had not taught him. Had she tried? Heinrich could not remember, but he returned home from Egypt to find both his sons had learned these skills. Heinrich was bewildered by Rudolf's shyness, the formality in his behavior, the seriousness of his speech -- when he did speak.

I was gone too long, Heinrich thought. *He has been warped by women.* He was glad when their Major walked up, hoping to give his greetings to Anna and have a word with Heinrich. "Ah, Mülner. That's not what we want to hear, is it?"

"Not us. No. But it does explain why I was ordered absolutely to prevent any tournaments today, though there are many who would have joined the tilt."

"Who enjoined you?"

"Von Schnabelberg. I suspected last night, but they," he gestured with disgust at the priests, "they offered nothing though they stayed at my house. These black robes can keep a secret. And, that's what I've come to ask…" He hesitated, looking at Anna.

"What?"

"They would stay some days at Castle Lunkhofen. I've come on their behalf to ask."

Heinrich wondered. Why didn't the Black Robes stay with the White Brothers? Why had they even stayed with the Mayor.? There was no way Heinrich could say no, though he could not imagine that they would not prefer to stay in town.

"Of course. If it is not too much trouble for you, bring them with you. I have my family here and horses to take back."

"I'll see to it, then. Where is the young Lord?"

Heinrich gestured with his head toward the square. "Listening."

"It would be well if you could keep your sons out of this. Outfit some other young man instead."

"There is nothing I would like more," Heinrich said, shaking his head. "Dine with us when you bring the friars. At least we can listen to their musicians."

Though she did not want the black robes to stay with them, Anna knew that she could not turn them away. Any passing guest, man or woman in need, could be the Lord Jesus Christ. She looked hard through the crowd until she found her sons. They were tall and healthy, those boys. It felt to her at times as if the lives of her small dead children had contributed to their strength and soundness of limb.

"I'm sorry, Anna," said Heinrich. "I know this isn't what you would have."

"No. I would have them as far away from my sons as possible."

"As would I. Perhaps they will not stay very long."

"They have stayed too long already," was her soft answer, after which she crossed herself.

Chapter 4, A Supper

The moment the family returned from the fair, Anna set the servants to prepare supper for the friars and anyone else who came by; she expected many would learn that the priests were staying at the castle and would want news. She then went to the chapel. When her husband left for the Holy Land, Anna had received permission to dedicate a private chapel to the Virgin in whose name the Teutonic Knights served. It was on the third floor of the tower, with double arched windows to the east for which Heinrich had brought glass. Its plastered walls were painted with pictures of the Holy Mother and Child along with the lives of Anna's favorite saints. On other walls hung tapestries embroidered with stories from the Bible. She lit a candle and surrendered her heart to prayer.

"Holy Mother of God," she began, "accept my small sacrifice and listen to my prayer. You lost your son. Your sorrow is the source of your compassion. Please, Holy Mother, the wars for the Holy City have done little but take our children and our husbands from us. But if Peace is not the desire of our Heavenly Father, Holy Mother, and my sons must go," she prayed, all the while thinking of Conrad, "keep them safe and return them to me."

She crossed herself but remained kneeling in the silence of the chapel, her mind wandering back to all the solitary hours she had passed in this room. The walls held all the prayers for her lost babies and for Heinrich, about whom she had heard nothing for years upon years. She did not know he was still alive until he crossed the threshold of his own castle. "Your father!" she had said in a hoarse whisper to Rudolf, who was sitting beside her.

Though minnesingers, wandering priests, merchants and knights came and went, news from the Holy Land was seldom particular. She had heard of the loss of Damietta, but had no idea if

Heinrich was there. She had heard the story of the little St. Francis from Italy standing up to al'Kamil on the battlefield, but there was nothing in that story to tell her if Heinrich was alive or if he had ever reached the Holy City. She knew nothing of the news she longed for. "Rest in the Lord," was the counsel offered by her priest. "His ways are mysterious, but they are always for our good. You should think of your husband's soul as pledged to his Heavenly Father. And this is your sacrifice as well. You will be together with our Lord Jesus Christ throughout eternity. Is there better comfort, my lady?"

Anna could not say no, but the comfort offered by eternity did not relieve the suffering she felt in the moment.

"Have more faith, my lady. The Lord God loves you. He will not cause anything that will harm you. Your suffering now is for your future salvation."

A popular song of the time came from Italy and was played often in Heinrich's hall during the years he was not there. Anna would ask for it, and that it be sung in Italian. All she knew was that Heinrich had gone with the Emperor's men; his last, and only, letter had come from Sicily. The song was told by a wife yearning for her beloved who had gone to fight the infidels. It seemed to come from Anna's own heart, and it eased her loneliness and expressed her anger.

Holy, Holy, Holy God
Who came to us in the Virgin
Watch over my love,
For you parted him from me,
O high, dread, fearful power
My sweet love
Be in your care…

The cross saves humanity
And makes me lose the way.
The cross fills me with grief,

I get no help praying to God.
O pilgrim cross,
Why have you destroyed me?
Alas, weary, wretched,
I burn and am all consumed.

She had confessed many times her anger at God for taking Heinrich from her; she had confessed her lack of faith. Each time she had met with the same response: "It is your salvation toward which you struggle now. As Herr Lunkhofen has taken up his cross, you must take yours with more confidence in our Heavenly Father. Pray for more faith. As penance, you must say one hundred fifty Our Fathers before prime tomorrow."

She never stopped there; certain she had not confessed all, she doubled and tripled the penance that it might bring Heinrich home safely. Beneath her gown she had tied a vest woven of jute and goat hair, hoping the physical misery she felt would remind her that Christ had suffered for her, but all it did was make her hope that the misery she felt somehow relieved Heinrich from misery he met with on the way. Now God wanted her sons.

"Mother!" Rudolf's surprised voice broke her reverie. "I," he stopped. He had seen his mother here often when he was a child, as she was now, tears streaming down her face, rosary in her hand. "What is it?"

"Perhaps nothing. I hope nothing." She looked straight into his eyes. He could not meet her gaze, knowing what it meant.

"Mother, I…"

"I know already. Talk to your father. Let him tell you what it is like." Her voice was bitter; with a fine edge of rage.

"Mother, it matters not at all to me what it is like."

"And for what?" She looked around, suddenly, at the paintings on her chapel walls, the brightly colored statues of the Virgin holding her small child on one arm, blessing all mankind with the other, as if to say, "Fear not. My Son and I will make it right for

39

you."

"This is not the place for this conversation, Rudolf, and perhaps it's a conversation for you to have with your father. Were you looking for me or have you come to pray?"

"I've come to talk to Brother Friedrich."

"He is not here. You will take the vow?"

"It's what I must do." Rudolf at that moment decided his future and spoke out.

"How can it be what you must do? Gretchen will be here soon; your life will begin. Your troth has been given her. You cannot wipe away one Holy vow to take another."

Rudolf looked away from her. He knew what this was doing to her; his hope lay in the knowledge – the belief – that without this he would do even worse. If he died on the journey – or in a battle – his death would make sense. If he remained where he was, tormented as he was, his death would hurt everyone who loved him, causing pain he would not cause if he could help it. To lie apart from the family, prayers unsaid, in unsanctified ground? His soul sundered from God and from all that he loved? That was impossible.

"Excuse me, my lady," he said to Anna. "May I?" Brother Friedrich announced his arrival with a soft cough.

"Certainly, Father, enter."

The friar took two steps into the chapel, and kneeling, crossed himself. He then came to the two and said to Rudolf, "You wanted to talk to me?"

"Can you leave us, Mother?"

Anna's eyes blazed for a moment and flashed fire at the Dominican. "Supper is soon, Rudolf," she said and left the chapel.

"What is it, my son, that you want to talk to me about?"

"Joining this crusade."

"Have you spoken with your parents?" asked the friar.

"Now, with my mother. I have not spoken with my father. I am to be married soon, and that was to be, for them – for me – the beginning of my life. Until this past spring I had not thought of anything else, but now…" Rudolf stopped.

"What happened in the spring?"

"Dozens of people were stranded here in the rain; among them were a minnesinger and his troupe. He sang about the Crusade, how a person would serve God and win his soul from Satan by fighting for the Cross. Gretchen – my bride – we were happy, but..."

"God is trying to reach you, my son. You must pay attention; to turn from your true path is the heaviest sin, because, in doing so, you refuse God's will for you."

Rudolf imagined his life as a labyrinthine network of forest trails, path turned to path, one leading here, the next one there. Which to choose? Who knew the forest well enough to point the way? And for him? Satan was everywhere, within every choice, and every decision; his false voice called out in the darkness – for there were many times when Rudolf had navigated through the forest in the dark of a moonless night. "How can anyone know his true path?"

"It's always the one that shines most brightly, so brightly sometimes that it arouses fear. 'Am I adequate to God's will?' we ask ourselves, never thinking that our Heavenly Father made nothing that is inadequate."

"My father will not like it."

"Your earthly father loves you, but his concern is mainly for your body and your happiness here on earth. It is the counsel of our Heavenly Father that you must seek. He is concerned with your soul."

Rudolf looked at his feet. "What should I do?"

"Pray, my son. God will show you. Feel no shame if He shows you that you must remain behind, and feel no pride if He should show you that you are chosen to fight for Him against the infidel. One way is not better than the other when you accede to God's will." Rudolf's face blanched. The friar knew then that this boy was deeply troubled, sad, perhaps frightened. "My son, do you want to confess?"

Rudolf's heart pounded. He could not expose himself yet. All that was in him was dark and mysterious, even to himself. If prayer would show him something of who he was and where to go, he would seek an answer there before confessing. "No, Father."

"By request of my lord, your father, I will hold Mass here at matins. If you wish to confess, come before Mass. I will be here. Wait a moment, and I will go with you down to supper." The friar went to the altar and knelt in prayer before the hanging painting of the crucified Christ.

Although for the moment Rudolf had kept his own counsel, he knew what was right already; he knew what was necessary. He knew his nature, how he had been made. He knew the terrible fires of Hell and he knew that God was offering him a boon, hope for a happy life and peaceful death. He knew he would go, but he was not yet ready to take the steps.

How can I drag Gretchen into the abyss that is my life? he wondered. *What sad father will I be to our children as I am? How can I know that I will not infect them with this terror, or that Satan is not waiting in my very seed to capture my children as they come into the world? And why can I not turn myself away from him?* He hoped to find a way to ask this priest those questions, but he was not ready.

***

A long table, covered with a white cloth, had been laid in the center of the hall. At one end sat Sir Heinrich and Anna. Along the sides sat Mayor Mülner and his wife, Duke von Schnabelberg and his Lady, the Dominicans, and their singers. Food was carried in from the kitchens across the courtyard: a whole roasted hind, soups, vegetables from Heinrich's gardens, a compote of fruit, pudding, roasted fowl, bread. There was wine and beer to wash everything down. The friars ate little, as their vows demanded. Before the food was cleared away, the singer and his troupe began to play, but the songs they chose now were not the rousing Crusading songs of that afternoon. They sang ballads; each song invoked the almost unspeakable yearning of mankind. And for what? Even that was beyond telling, though it was named love:

My heart and my body want to separate,

That have ridden together all my life.
The body wants to strike against the heathen,
But the heart has chosen out a woman
Before all the world. It has weighed on me ever since,
That one will not go in the steps of the other.
My eyes have brought me to grief.
May God alone break up the strife.

I had hoped to be free of this great weight
When I took the cross for the glory of God.
It would be right if the heart were in it too,
But its own faith held it back.
I would truly be a living man again
If it would stop its ignorant desiring,
I see how, to the heart, it is all one
How I shall fare at last.

When the Dominicans rose and excused themselves, all in the room seemed to breathe a sigh of great relief. In front of the friars, they had curbed the expression of their thoughts. Now they could speak, and they did. Anna apprehensively watched her sons.

"Stop," said Heinrich suddenly, motioning to the musicians. "Let us have music without words, and that softly. Your songs are…" He stopped. "My guests, have not the singers taxed their voices enough for the evening? We should not take all their livelihood!"

His guests nodded; Anna was greatly relieved.

"How can they tell the truth of it when they don't know? And he in Rome? What does he know, either? One hand washes the other. It was for this our Emperor refused to fight and for that was excommunicated. How can you attack the men with whom you trade?" Mayor Mülner looked as if he might explode. "The streets of Venice are lined with stolen gold. What interest had they in making war, except against Christians in Byzantium? None, except that it could make them more wealthy, but we, guileless Germans, fall easily into the trap. Is it not enough that we pay their bills? It is the fault of His Holiness. He is a pawn of the French."

"Ah, Mülner, best not to bring the Holy Father into the discussion," advised the Duke.

"Talk about this without bringing the Holy Father into the discussion? He *is* the discussion. The wealth of Rome is carried on the back of the German people. Is it not sung, 'Look at the women, what they wear on their heads, and proud knights clothed in peasant dress.' It is everywhere. The times are bad, and it is because all we make goes to Rome to make these endless crusades so wealthy men and kings can build their fortunes. Our Emperor? Excommunicated, not by one Pope, but by two. For what? Because he treated with the Saracen and won peace for ten years without shedding blood – and now?"

"Calm yourself, Mülner. Clearly this touches you, but the affairs of the world need not touch us here tonight. Our host has fed us well; his lady is serene and happy with him by her side. Her sons sit here in the hall with us. This is not the moment for ranting anger." The Duke strove to keep peace, to alert Mülner that his words were causing pain where pain need not be.

"What do you think those Dominicans are doing here? You think it is to keep Lunkhofen's sons here with their mother?" Mülner had hit a nerve. "No. It is because Lunkhofen here can pay to outfit his sons; it will not cost the Pope anything, and they can go with their father's proud horses to the same battlefield where he," Mülner gestured toward Heinrich with a nod of his head, "and I saw what should not be seen. We walked through the gates of Hell, I swear to you."

Heinrich was stunned for the moment. The words were out; Mülner would break this tense illusion of peace. He was a forceful, practical man. Heinrich knew this, as he had known Mülner all his life. He saw things as they were and he spoke them as he saw them.

"Have you seen this, my lord Duke?" Mülner could not be stopped. "Were you at Damietta where we walked through the streets filled with the dead? Children, women, old men, some died starving, nothing left of them but stretched skin across an awkward frame; others? Who knows? But the stench – my God, awful beyond belief, and when the battle started, and blood soaked the dry crust of the earth, we walked. Those of us who survived walked out in red mud above our ankles, kicking pieces of men out of the way."

Heinrich looked at the mayor and shook his head almost imperceptibly, but Mülner kept on. "And these Black Robes? They come into town and promise salvation to those who take the cross. It doesn't matter what any Roman Pope decides; he's been told by God. That is no road to Heaven. I tell you, any man who seeks salvation in that way is damned. God can want nothing to do with him."

The hall was stunned silent. All knew that Duke von Schnabelberg – though a high-ranking Teutonic knight, a Landkommtur -- had served the cross on the Baltic front where victory was easy, the distances short, the dangers comparatively few. It was a crusade against the barbarian infidel northeast of the Rhine, above the Danube. Unlike the Saracen, their fortifications were primitive, their weapons soft and their willingness to surrender more common than a willingness to fight. The Duke had been insulted in Heinrich's hall, and the company was unsure what would happen. This was not courtesy. In the old days, this would not have happened, but in the old days, Mülner would not be dining at a lord's table like this. These new times were creating new lords out of old commoners.

Von Schnabelberg stood and with him his wife. "Sir Heinrich," he said, "I will take my leave. I understand the concerns of our mayor, and I understand his anger. Do not let what he has said here concern you any more than it concerns me. It is not for we of noble birth to tell such as he how to behave at table in his lord's castle. In the end, breeding is all, as you know with your beautiful horses." In this way, the Duke returned the insult. He set Mayor Mülner, for all his having been knighted and a landowner, apart from the rest of the company and established that to fight with him would be beneath his dignity. Though the old aristocracy was – as the singers had observed – declining in wealth and power, it was not yet gone. Heinrich and Anna followed the Duke and his lady to the immense door that made an island of safety of the castle tower.

"I beg your pardon, my lord," said Mülner on Heinrich's return to the table. "It is difficult for me to sit silent when…"

"Leave it, Mülner. You are right. He was not there, but it was wrong of you to insult anyone under my roof."

"For that I apologize." Mülner bowed low before his childhood friend.

Heinrich sighed. It had been a horribly long day. The wine he had drunk sat uncomfortably on his head; he was filled with a foggy mass of melancholy and could not think clearly. His wife was distracted and afraid she would lose her sons; for this she would reproach him as if he had sought out the Dominicans and their Papal orders and brought them to Appletree Village himself. His sons? He would have to talk to them, each of them, and with neither would it be an easy conversation. He doubted he could stop them; the stakes were high, the soul again on the table to be played. He feared that rather than hosting a wedding, he would be outfitting both boys for Palestine.

Chapter 5, Sons

Brother Friedrich rose when the moon was still high and went to the chapel to prepare for Mass, hoping to talk again to Rudolf. He had seen troubled young men all his life, in his wanderings, in confession, in the monasteries where he lived when he was not traveling doing God's work. Many such entered the brotherhood hoping to find peace by relinquishing the world, believing the world itself to be their torment, only to learn that they carried their suffering within themselves. Then the problems began; how to combat the self for the sake of the soul? These tormented priests undertook extraordinary acts of penance to combat Satan. Some never slept for fear of Satan entering their open mouths in the night; others spent hours on their knees repeating Our Father to keep evil thoughts away. Others beat themselves fiercely, appearing at Mass with their cassocks stuck to the bloody crusts on their backs or legs. Some fashioned belts of green thorn branches and as the branches dried, shriveled and shrank, the thorns tore ever more deeply into the soft flesh. Only in death were they sure of relief through the rite of extreme unction. Brother Friedrich wondered if Rudolf might be one of these. If Rudolf were struggling against Satan, he needed help from the church, and for this, Brother Friedrich hoped he would appear and confess, but that early morning there came before the priest a very different boy.

After listening to the discussions and to the minnesingers, Conrad was unable to sleep. He burned with restlessness and struggled to call it the longing for God. His youth and health argued against the rather morbid fear of death that turned upon the wheel of fortune. The need for salvation seemed so far away; he acknowledged its reality, yet it did not drive him. What drove him was curiosity, the wish for glory – and wanderlust. When the sun began to lighten the sky, Conrad arose and went in search of Brother

Friedrich.

"Father? Can I speak to you?"

Brother Friedrich looked up. Instead of Rudolf, here stood this young animal. Brother Friedrich had to smile. "You are Conrad, am I right?"

"Yes."

"I am free now unless someone comes seeking confession. You can help me with Mass if you will; you can serve as my altar boy."

"If it pleases you, Father."

In Conrad the priest recognized the gleaming-eyed ferocity of young men who throw themselves against the world to take their own measure. His life would be a treasure quest. If he lived long enough, the end might well be God.

"Father, I want to go to Jerusalem."

"Why?" The priest knew the boy was seeking the friar's advocacy with his parents.

"To serve Christ. To save Jerusalem."

"Do you go for the love of God or the longing for adventure? The second is love of the self. You must know why you are going if you would reach the Kingdom of Heaven in this way."

Conrad was silent. These points were too shadowy for him. God troubled him little. He woke in the morning and attended prayers with all the devotion of which he was capable. He confessed often enough, believed in forgiveness and tried to do right as far as he understood it. He had little awareness of the subtlety of sin. The stories of saints commanded by God to wander the world interested him most. For Conrad, they were stories of adventure.

The friar was sure this boy would go. His eager look demanded that the world come out and show itself. Strong and active, Conrad was a perfect recruit. Still, the friar did not want to make it easy. Unless he could be sure Conrad could merge his identity with that of the group, join the knights in their lives of chastity and poverty, the friar would try to persuade him not to go. It was not an easy life, and the world was large and filled with fabulous temptations. There was pain on the journey, great danger; the commitment had to be complete and wholehearted, or the expense of going would prove to be useless. The Friar believed the boy had the makings of a Crusading knight, but he wanted to be certain that Conrad understood completely that it would mean complete obedience always to the Rule and those above him in rank.

"Consider if you can make this journey for the love of God, as if you do not even exist except as a tool of His glory."

Conrad nodded, suddenly feeling that he was on the brink of something immense, somber and dangerous, and if he could not assent, he would regret it his entire life.

"I can."

"Then I will confess you. Are you ready?"

Conrad's heart pounded. Could he do this without his father's permission? "Father," he began, "I must talk to my father. I cannot do this without his knowledge, but I will do it."

Far from displeasing the friar, Conrad's response showed the manner of man he was; he would serve the Brotherhood and God well.

"That is how it should be. After you have spoken with him, come to me. Now, help me with the Mass; the bell will be rung for matins very soon."

They unfolded the white linen cloth and covered the altar. Over this was placed a smaller covering of purple brocade embroidered with a cross of gold. The chalice and dishes were set out along with a small golden bell. The host, which had been blessed by the Holy Father in Rome, was kept in a silver casket beneath the altar. Conrad opened this small storehouse and removed the tray. Just as they finished, the bells in the courtyard rang, and soon Heinrich and Anna appeared, dismayed to see their son helping the Dominican, knowing what this portended. They knelt at the doorway, crossed themselves and entered in silence. Rudolf came, followed by various members of the household staff.

"*In nomine Patris, et Filii, et Spiritus Sancti,*" began the friar, and in those few Latin words all present accepted the inevitability of the future though they knew they would still resist, resistance being an element of the same inevitability. God's will would be done.

***

"My lord!" Anna called out from the hall, seeing Heinrich crossing the courtyard and walking toward the stables. "Heinrich. Wait."

Heinrich turned. "Ah, Anna."

She had run after him and now stood beside him, her pale face drawn, dark circles under her eyes.

"Have you spoken with him?"

"Conrad?"

"No, no, it's Rudolf that worries me. Have you spoken with him?"

"Rudolf? Rudolf will not go, surely. He is engaged. He seems to love Gretchen." He shook his head. "This whole thing," Heinrich made a gesture with his gloved hand, "this whole thing fills me with dread, Anna. I do not like it."

She needed to know this; she needed to know that he would not encourage either boy to leave.

"You don't know him as I do. He will go. Love won't keep him here, either."

"*I* had no choice, Anna."

"It was just so hard. The children were so small, and I was only a little older than Gretchen. I was so often frightened."

"It was years ago, Anna. I have not left you since."

There was silence between them. This was an old wound and a perpetual discussion. Heinrich then said, "Has Rudolf spoken to you? He has not spoken to me. Sooner or later, he will have to."

"He is not like you, Heinrich, nor is he like Conrad. He takes things hard very hard. He feels too much. He is often downcast, and I cannot fathom why."

"It's clear to me. You have infected him with your brooding and your religion."

"Brooding? Religion? How would I have survived without the love of our dear Lord and his blessed Mother? You were not here."

"You can turn this around if you want to, Anna, but when I left, you were a warm and loving wife. I returned to a home that had the feel of a convent."

"It was a convent."

Heinrich had heard this before. That there had been no children born since his return some five years past spoke all it had to. She lay with him, yes, but took no pleasure in it and for this? No children. How could that be God's will?

"It IS a convent," he said and walked away from her. He loved her, but in her house of bitterness and guilt, there was no room for him. If she had more children, what she faced now would be easier for her, or so he thought. She would, at least, not have everything resting on these two boys if she had a house filled with children's voices and their games.

Heinrich knew he had to find Rudolf. It was unlikely he'd be in the stable and equally unlikely he'd be on the green riding or training horses. He did his work, and did it well, but never with the excitement Conrad seemed to feel when a horse registered its acceptance of what it was being taught. Conrad was moved by the beauty of a horse and delighted in the coming of foals, anticipating how the new horse would look and pleased when his conjectures came out right. Thinking of his younger boy, Heinrich went to the stables anyway.

"Conrad, I would have a word."

"As would I, father."

Heinrich reached for one of the two brushes in his son's hands. "Here, I'll help you brush down this mare while we talk. She did well for us this year, did she not?" She had given them a flawless bay colt. "Conrad, I know you've decided to go. I cannot stop you, but I would. The times are hard enough and dangerous. In spite of the songs of the minnesingers, it is no glorious journey. No one wins those battles. The land belongs to the infidel. He is there in droves; his life is there, his land, his family, his crops and animals. He will be there after we have long given up and returned to our own business." Heinrich looked at his young son and thought, but did not say, "You cannot hear me."

"How can you say that, father? Jerusalem belongs to the followers of Christ!"

"Many who live there are followers of Christ. They do not need to fight; they need only believe. And they do; they have for centuries."

Heinrich's discussion was too subtle for Conrad. He did not want to remain, but if he were obliged, he would. He was simply hungry for life. Stories of chivalry awakened in him a longing for danger, for the chance to prove himself against a worthy foe. He had practiced the arts of knighthood from the time he was able to run and play with other boys.

His mother drew him to her to learn the gentler arts; he was quick enough learning to read and to write, but he preferred to be outdoors. He trained falcons and hunting hawks and spent hours in the woods with bow and arrow, bringing home venison and wild pig. When his father returned, Conrad entered wholeheartedly into the business of breeding horses. Such a boy should want adventure.

"Mayor Mülner spoke out of place in front of Duke von Schnabelberg, but he described what we saw. This," he gestured around the stable, "is your calling. Have your own family, breed and train horses. It is your gift, son."

"When I return I can do those things."

Heinrich was silent for some time, then softly said, "I can't stop you, then."

"I will do as I am bid."

"Much expense is involved, Conrad. I will need to outfit you; you will need three horses, one to ride across the land, one on which to fight, and one to carry your burdens. Ten servants to ride with you, their expenses as well.

Conrad wondered if this were permission or argument. "Are you saying I can go, father?"

"I'm saying I cannot in conscience stop you, and perhaps if you go, your brother… What of Rudolf?" asked Heinrich.

Conrad nodded.

"He has said as much to you?"

"He has been looking for an answer to his questions."

"What questions? Why can't he come to me with his questions?"

"Rudolf's questions are strange, and I don't understand them. Perhaps the black robe does. Rudolf doesn't know how…" Conrad stopped.

"How what?"

"To speak to you, Father."

"I am his father. He need only come to me."

"It is not so simple for Rudolf; nothing is."

"Ah," sighed Heinrich. "You, I understand. Rudolf? That he would want to go seems strange to me. He has no real interest in battle. I thought he looked forward to his marriage."

"Rudolf's reasons are his reasons. You will have to talk to him. I imagine he is trying to decide for himself his own right course."

"And this wandering friar will help with that? He has his own interests!"

"What?"

"Nothing. Nothing, son. You are right. What is between Rudolf and me is not your concern."

Heinrich was only expressing his sense of hopeless frustration with his family. Seven years he had been gone, six years back, and he still could not find them. Who were they? They often seemed stranger to him than the infidels with whom he had lived in Egypt.

"Rudolf is coming," said Conrad, looking up. Heinrich stood on the far side of the horse from the doorway. Conrad knew his brother was avoiding his father, and if he had seen him would not have come in.

Rudolf rushed in, his eyes frantic. "Conrad, can we…" Rudolf then saw Heinrich. "Father." He choked out the word.

"We're just brushing down this mare, son. Sit or grab a brush." Rudolf stood a moment, as if exposed, and then sat on a stool some distance from his father. The stable was silent, but Heinrich could have plucked his son's unspoken words from the air above them. "Rudolf, I know. I know what you are puzzling over," said Heinrich, finally.

Rudolf blushed red. Did his father know why?

"I would join the crusade, father."

"I want you here, married to Gretchen. I want you safe for your mother and for your wife. Do you understand me?"

"I do, father, and because of that I have not spoken." Rudolf looked at the ground. He felt his heart would burst of its own necessity. "Father, if I am to live in Schneebeli's castle, to be lord, to be husband to Gretchen, I must go."

"You make no sense. To be a husband to Gretchen you must be here."

"I cannot, father. There – this – I must do first."

"Why? You go risk a life for what is yours already? Listen well. Most men die and many of them without ever seeing the Holy Land. The priests, the minnesingers don't tell you this. I can tell you what it is like. You – for your soul – would choose Hell. You would choose Hell with Heaven in your hand." Heinrich motioned around the stable, a gesture that was meant to show Rudolf all the world.

"Would you have stayed?"

"You have a choice."

"No, Father, I do not."

"Who – or what – is forcing you? Is it Gretchen? Have the songs put this into her mind? She seems to love you too well to wish you away from her."

"It is not Gretchen, Father. Were it she, I would not go. I would reason with her."

"What is it?"

"I cannot say."

"You'd better, or I will think you have no thought for others."

"I must go for the good of my soul, Father. If I do not go, I don't want to imagine…"

"What are you talking about?"

"If I go, all my sins will be absolved. I will be washed clean and can begin as a new man, a better man, with Gretchen, with you and mother."

"What sins can you have committed that you must risk such consequences?"

"I do not know." Rudolf wanted to run from his father, but there was no way. Heinrich stood between him and the door.

For all he found his oldest son incomprehensible, Heinrich could see that Rudolf's pain was real. Each moment it became more difficult for him to hide it. "The Friars are not here for you; they are here for Conrad, or so I was told by Mülner."

Conrad looked at his father. Of this he had known nothing.

"It is not them, Father, it is ME. There is something in ME." He felt he was a child having a bad dream, crying out to his father for help in the dark of night. Rudolf fell into a fit of sobbing. Heinrich was stunned that his silent, stoical, mature and careful son would expose such a core of emotion. Conrad, from time to time, lost his temper, and all heard a momentary clap of thunder in a sunny day, but Rudolf? He held himself to himself, appearing calm and masterful, older than his years. Heinrich had seen men break down this way at the approach of the enemy or the sight of balls of fire jettisoned from catapults. The first moment of the battle unnerved many who saw before them all the fearsome gore of Hell. But then, most rallied and fought, some of them, just to end it one way or another. Heinrich had never before seen a man respond like this at the prospect of NOT going to war. "Rudolf, calm yourself. This is no way to behave. It is unmanly. What has put you in this state? Is it the priest and his tales of Hell, of torment? Has he made you fear what will happen if you do not go? He is wrong in that. Our Heavenly Father does not require you to join the crusade. It is not every man's path."

Again the word "path." Why did not God lay in front of a man the one road he should take? Why had He made life an intricate network of decisions, each one carrying unknown and often terrible consequences? Rudolf wiped his eyes on his sleeve and took a deep breath before he quietly answered, "I know that, Father. But I believe it is mine."

Heinrich felt a cold hand grab his heart. His boys would go, and he would be left alone with Anna, who would probably grow more bitter and angry with the boys gone. She would blame him. He shuddered.

"Rudolf, there is no reason for you to go. Conrad will go; it is enough. The Holy Father expects nothing more from this family. The defense of our home is no small matter, as you know. I forbid any more talk of this. Conrad will go and you will stay. That is the end of it."

Heinrich walked out of the stable, wondering how he could tell Anna he had failed, and she would be left again.

Friar Friedrich's writing desk was an interesting contraption. He could sling it over his shoulder or across his back in his travels and within it carry parchment and dry inks, a selection of quills already cut, and a penknife. He was so dependent on it that at times he wondered if it did not pose a danger to his soul. Just now he was sitting with it propped on his knee, putting together a message to the Bishop of Constanz about the difficulty of raising a fighting force out of the disillusioned, fragmented remains of Frederick II's empire and the eager, forceful Habsburg family and its allies. He looked up to see Rudolf in the doorway.

"Am I disturbing you, Father?" Rudolf blushed bright red, then blanched white.

"Naturally not. I am at your disposal."

"Can we talk? Can we talk in confidence?"

"Do you wish to confess?"

"Father, I am not looking for God's forgiveness. I'm looking for an answer."

"An answer to whether you go or not rests in the space between you and God."

"Not that answer, Father."

"All right. Tell me."

"I am afraid." Rudolf was shaking; he had never spoken of this.

"Of what?"

"God has cast me aside."

"Why?"

"There are times, Father, when the light is extinguished within my heart, and I cannot find God anywhere."

"How come these times?"

"Of themselves. There is no cause. I have seen something like this in my mother. During the time my father was gone and there was no word of him, she lived in dread and uncertainty. That was clear and honest grief, fear of having lost what she loved most, but these times come on me with no such reason, and I feel I have been buried alive." Rudolf fought to hold his tears. "The feeling holds me in thrall. I feel nothing. I am numb. What once delighted me, does not affect me. I feel I am a corpse, empty of human sensation, my only feeling a sadness that will not lift."

"You must pray."

"It's difficult to pray. I feel as if, forgive me," Rudolf crossed himself, "there is no God and everything is a lie."

"You must pray, however difficult. Only God can lift such darkness."

"I pray, but," Rudolf stopped. "I want to die. If I sleep, I have nightmares. I awaken with that horrible presence all around me. There is no escape, and another day will pass like that, and another, and then another. I rouse myself for the sake of my mother, but I would not were it myself alone."

"The worst sin of all is to take the life God has given you."

"I know that, Father."

"You must examine your soul. Find this sin and bring it to the surface."

"Try as I might, I cannot see what sin I have committed to bring me this torment. I have thought and fasted and prayed, Father, to find the answer, but I have not found it."

"You fear Satan is inside you."

Rudolf broke down. This was his fear. He feared he would be tortured forever for a crime he didn't know.

"Satan is not inside you, my son, but he is doing what he can to weaken you from outside. When you reach the point where you can take your own life, Satan has nearly won. You must fight him, young lord."

"How? Each time he gets stronger. I am always afraid that each happy moment is a trap. I can go to bed at night filled with peace, and awaken to find the darkness returned."

"If you knew that your soul was forever safely in God's custody, would you still be afraid?"

"No."

"And you wish to go on Crusade for your soul's safety?"

"Yes, Father."

"That is the highest motive. To go on Crusade is to throw yourself completely into the arms of God. Come what may, you risk your life for the Cross, sure of the Kingdom of Heaven."

"Yes."

"You wonder, 'Will it work?'"

"Yes, Father."

"You are suspicious. That is Satan working again. You should have complete trust in the words of our Holy Father in Rome. God has shown him that the gates of Heaven are open to those who fight for the cross."

"That is not what I doubt, Father. I doubt Satan will ever leave me alone. Why me? Why does he think I am one who could be swayed to him? Does this not show that I am one who could be swayed?"

"Ah, God does not test the weak. He knows their dimensions. He tests the strong, those he loves most. Satan cannot reach those whom God has fashioned as little more than simple animals; those are God's chosen children. There are others whom God has chosen. It would seem you are one of these."

"*This* is a sign of God's love?"

"All of life is a sign of God's love."

Rudolf was silent.

"What will you do, young lord? Have you spoken with your father?"

"Just now. He forbade me to leave."

"He cannot stop you."

"My mother . . .," Rudolf could not hold back his tears. "My mother suffered greatly when my father was gone, and now Conrad and I will go."

"Your father is here with her."

"Still, I can see how to her it does not seem fair."

"God's justice is not man's justice. God's justice is absolute, all encompassing, immense, to us, inscrutable."

"I am to be married, Father."

"So I have been told."

"I must think of her."

"How can you give your life to her when you are in this desperate struggle?"

"That is my question."

"Best to resolve your fears first, then go to her free and unencumbered. Love between a man and a woman is part of God's infinite plan, but that you live in peace and happiness is God's blessing. You do not now live in peace with yourself."

"That's true." Rudolf had not expected to be so understood. Still, he felt suddenly exhausted.

"My great fear has been that Satan was inside of me. You have helped me."

"You are not out of danger. He is trying with all his might to win your soul."

"Yes."

"To fight for the Cross will build a fortress that Satan can never breach. You will be free."

"Can you talk to my father for me? Can you explain all these things so he will understand? I tried, but when I looked into his eyes, I knew he would fear for me and be angered at me. I did not expect him to understand."

"Sir Heinrich has certainly seen things you cannot imagine and would naturally rather you stayed home, but," the friar paused, "he does not seem the kind of man to be tortured by feelings such as yours. They would seem strange to him."

"Have you been on crusade, Father?"

"I went on a pilgrimage to Jerusalem during the truce. Even then there was no peace. You will see things, young lord, that will challenge everything you know, but in those challenges, you will find relief from the turmoil inside your heart. They may be forgotten in that more difficult struggle. I will go this time, soon after I leave here. The Holy Father is sending me so that I can report to him what happens, how things are between the brotherhoods of knights who fight among themselves, doing the work of the Saracens for them." The friar sighed. "Such futility," he said, "that among Christians there is no peace."

***

"Marry first, Rudolf, please," said Anna. "Give Gretchen a son to hold next to her heart while you are far away."

"Mother, how much comfort was I to you when father was away?"

"That is beside the point."

"No. That is the point. Father's absence was difficult for you, more difficult, I am sure, because you had to care for Conrad and me."

"Your father's absence was very difficult for me. That's true. But it would have been worse if I had been alone with no children to care for and love. You must marry first."

"I cannot. I have taken the vow, and I must remain chaste until I return. It is easier to remain what I am than to return to what I was. Mother, what if I do not return?"

"Do not go! The Holy Father has given us ways to fulfill this duty without your going. Your brother is going; your father can find someone to go in your stead. It will amount to the same thing."

"No other person can fulfill my vows to God. Even if that is what the Holy Father's document says, surely such a choice is there for the man who becomes ill or for other real reasons cannot keep his vow, not for me."

"Go away, Rudolf. I cannot reason with you. You want to turn the dagger that pierced my heart when your father left. What have I done that I must always lose what I love most?"

"Father returned, Mother."

"But much was lost that can never be regained."

"That is why I will not marry now, Mother. I don't want Gretchen to spend her life sorrowful and bitter if I don't come back or even if I do."

Anna could not bear it. She turned her head away from him and said, "Leave me, Rudolf. I don't want to see you. Leave."

He stood where he was in the great hall, empty but for the two of them. He did not know where he found the courage, but he did not budge.

"Did you hear me?"

"Mother, please hear me out. I'm not Conrad. Wandering in distant lands is no dream of mine. I must go so I can love Gretchen, be a better son to you and father, be the lord of Schneebeli's lands when my time comes, that is if Gretchen is still free when I return, and wants me. I cannot do these things now, not as I should, not as I would do them."

"What stops you?"

"Satan."

She crossed herself at the sound of the word, and pulled back. That it could come so easily from her son's lips frightened her.

"Mother, for a long time I've been afraid that Satan is inside me. Brother Friedrich explained to me how I am in a battle with Satan as was St. Anthony. Do you recall his bitter fight in the desert?"

"You'd have me think you are a saint, Rudolf? May God forgive your pride."

"No, mother. Of course not. But sometimes the Evil One puts his cold hand around my heart, and the world is black. I find no joy, nothing of what I know of the world. This goes on for a long time and then he's gone. Brother Friedrich understood exactly when I told him; he explained everything to me. By going to Jerusalem, by taking the Cross for our Lord, I will cast Satan far, far away from me forever. He will never be able to come near me again, and I will be free."

Anna never imagined that below the sweet, calm surface of this boy, on whom she had relied for her own support, was such an abyss of dread.

Chapter 6, Decisions

Rudolf and his father rode toward the big house of Sir Adelbert. "You cannot do this for me, Father. If I do not talk to her, she will think I simply left her; she will not know why."

"Rudolf, how could I attempt to explain your insane behavior to that poor girl? Justify why you are breaking her heart when I can't begin to fathom it? Do you think she will understand any better than I? She won't. You are casting aside a sweet girl who loves you, breaking a vow, rejecting a cherished family alliance and for what? No. I'm coming along because I must talk to Schneebeli."

"My soul, Father."

"Your soul. You could well fear for your soul after this cruel business is over. You know what my leaving did to your mother."

Rudolf could only nod. There was no dispute there.

"At least," Heinrich continued, "you are wise – or kind – enough not to marry first."

Sir Adelbert's house was built close against hillside so it was easy to defend and reachable from only one direction. Heinrich and Adelbert, nicknamed "Schneebeli" — snowball — because of his pure, white hair — were cousins, brothers in their affection and rivalry. Rudolf had lived with Sir Adelbert and his family for three years as Adelbert's page, learning the skills of knighthood and service and falling in love with Gretchen, to whom he had been long engaged. In a family ceremony in Sir Adelbert's hall, Rudolf had been knighted by a blow from Sir Adelbert's hand. Soon after, his engagement to Gretchen had been announced at a party held by his father.

A track ran through the forest from Heinrich's castle and dropped into one of Schneebeli's large apple orchards. Workmen in the section of the orchard nearest the woods, seeing Heinrich and

Rudolf, ran to alert Sir Adelbert, who was working farther down.

"Heinrich! Rudolf! Welcome, welcome! What brings you?"

"This one," Heinrich said, gesturing behind him toward Rudolf. Though he tried to conceal it, his voice carried confusion, anger and dismay.

"He misses the girl, does he?" Sir Adelbert laughed. "Were we different, Heinrich?"

"*Quite* different," said Heinrich, shaking his head.

Rudolf dismounted slowly, weighed down by what he had come to do. The only way he could bear it was thinking of how, on his return from the Holy Land, he would be free of Satan's reach. *I will serve God*, he thought to himself. *I will serve God, and then I need no longer fear Satan.*

"Young Rudolf!" said Sir Adelbert, clapping Rudolf on the shoulder. "You seem downcast for a man about to see his bride!"

Gretchen and her mother were in the great hall sitting at their embroidery frames, sewing Gretchen's trousseau linens. Gretchen sat calmly working on the delicate stitches that were to be part of their marriage bed. She smiled at Rudolf; that he was there was a marvelous surprise to her. Rudolf stood without moving. Looking at her eyes, so filed with trust and love, his heart leapt to his throat. What was he doing? Everything would be all right after he had talked to her. He would be free from this burden of guilt.

He had rehearsed his words over and over. *Gretchen, please understand*, he always began in his mind. *Please understand that I do not want to go, but I must go and I must go for the sake of our happiness.*

Often, in his imagination, Gretchen understood him perfectly. He envisioned her reaching for his hand and saying, *I understand, Rudolf. Go. I will wait here for you.* At other times, he imagined her breaking down in tears and reproaching him for having no feelings.

A table was laid and food brought in. Hospitality expressed before business. The late summer light streamed through the open doorway. The tapestries moved slightly in the breeze making the men and women stitched into them seem to dance. Rudolf could not eat and could not look at Gretchen.

The two fathers went outside. Gretchen's mother, sure that Rudolf wanted to be alone with Gretchen, excused herself and went into an adjoining room where she could watch the two without interfering. She'd seen Rudolf's agitation; his need to speak was clear. She knew him to be complicated and intense and hoped that the sweet, open simplicity of her daughter would be a cheerful foil to Rudolf's darker moods.

Rudolf spoke softly, holding Gretchen's right hand. Gretchen cried out but did not draw her hand away. Rudolf stroked it as if it were a kitten. From this one sound the mother caught the sad gist of the conversation.

"Cannot we marry first?" Gretchen asked between small, choking sobs. "Then I would know that you are mine, that our future is ours. Perhaps I would have a child and your being away would be more bearable if I held him in my arms."

"No, it wouldn't, Gretchen. Believe me; I know."

"But if you do not return?"

"You would then be free as you are free now."

"What are you saying, Rudolf?"

"I know my decision has hurt you. I would not make it worse. If we break our betrothal now, your life will not change." These were the words his father had advised. Rudolf wanted to Gretchen to decide for herself if she would remain betrothed to him, if she would wait.

"I want my life to change!" Tears flowed afresh down her pale cheeks.

Rudolf nodded. Conrad, Gretchen and he all wanted their lives to change, while the old men, such as his father, insisted otherwise, and the old women wept over the past, saying, "Leave things be. They are fine as they are."

"My love, I must end the torment in my soul before beginning a life with you."

"Tormented, Rudolf? By what?"

"I can't explain. Just know that if I could find another way, I would."

"In my heart you are my husband," she said, sobbing. "Am I not your wife?"

"Yes." Rudolf's throat caught as he spoke.

"You may be killed!"

"I would not have you a widow, Gretchen, or our child an orphan."

Outside the two fathers had their discussion, and decided the betrothal would be broken. Heinrich spoke openly about his son's problems, his lack of stability; he painted a picture of a man who was less than ideal as a husband for a girl of Gretchen's simplicity and sweetness.

"If it could be Conrad, well, that would be different," said Heinrich. "But he is too young to marry and he is going, too. Adelbert, my brother, your little Gretchen must be free."

Sir Adelbert knew Rudolf well. He thought the boy's long moments of slanted melancholy were just part of youth, romantic yearning made worse by popular ballads and the stories that were passed around and sung everywhere. Listening to Heinrich, Sir Adelbert wondered if Rudolf would ever be a good husband to Gretchen. That Rudolf's moods could have a deeper, more frightening cause was more than unsettling. He crossed himself, fearing for his daughter's happiness. Such melancholy could erupt in many ways. Perhaps the boy was wise in deciding to ride away now, unmarried, for the good of his soul.

"When he comes back," said Sir Adelbert so as not to hurt his friend, "and if Gretchen is still free, and still wants him, we will simply start again."

"Do not hinder her on Rudolf's account, Adelbert," said Heinrich. "If it mattered to him as it should, he would not leave."

Father and son rode home in silence. Rudolf was furious, but he had no idea how to talk to his father. Finally, when he could bear the pressure of his rage no longer, he asked, "How can you have decided for us?"

"Rudolf, what would you have me do?"

"She could decide. I gave it to her to decide to wait for me or not."

"That is unfair. Is she to stand in front of you – whom she loves – and think practically about her future? What if she said to you that she did not want to wait, that youth is a fleeting moment, and hers could be gone before you returned? How would you feel then? And would you stay? No. You made this decision, not I."

Rudolf wanted Gretchen to wait, but he believed he deserved the pain he would feel if she told him that she would marry someone else instead of waiting for him.

"It is hers to say, Father, not yours."

"But you would leave her," argued Heinrich. "You may not return; most do not. Even if you return, you will be away longer than you know. Let her marry elsewhere. Likely she will be past marrying age when you return. Since you will not marry first, let her go free. Do you want to change your mind? Remain here for Gretchen?"

"I cannot, Father."

"Then let her go. It will hurt her less to follow her father's will than her own. She can accuse him now in her broken heart, but she will thank him later when her first child is born."

Chapter 7, Knighthood

At summer's end, instead of a wedding, there were investiture ceremonies so that Rudolf and Conrad could leave before the alpine passes were closed by snow. Conrad had not imagined during the wet days of spring, his heart stirred by a crusading song, that only six months later he would be measured for chain mail. Rudolf, sitting beside Gretchen in his father's castle on a rainy day, listening to the Minnesinger, could not have imagined that Gretchen's father would be handing him the reins to a gray warhorse rather than the hand of his daughter.

"All turns on the wheel of fate. There is nothing I can do to stop either of you short of locking you up." Heinrich shuddered. "Only, please God, you return."

"We will, Father. You worry too much," said Conrad, absolutely confident.

"That you do not know. But remember. Before you turn away from Castle Lunkhofen, take time to look and press it on your memory because you may never see it again."

Duke von Schnabelberg, on hearing of the decisions of Heinrich's sons, stepped forward to sponsor Conrad. The boy had impressed him with his vibrant, soul-sure youth and the passion he felt for the horse he had trained. Von Schnabelberg had great respect for Heinrich, and his heart was moved at the thought of both boys leaving their home. It was a grand thing, no doubt. Though Mayor Mülner had spoken out of turn, he had spoken truth that Duke von Schnabelberg could not deny. The journey ahead of the boys was long and dangerous; to go to war meant men would die. There was every chance Heinrich would lose both sons, but Conrad's restlessness was beautiful to von Schnabelberg. He, too, had longed to go, and when his moment had come, nothing could have held him back.

As a young man Conrad's age, von Schnabelberg had followed the Teutonic knights into the dark forests of pagan Prussia. He could still see that white on white world, snow, fog, ice-laden trees, the horse's white breath as they moved slowly between the trees on a road that was barely a track, no sound but that breath, the creaking of saddles, and the horse's soft footfall. Beneath white skies and falling snow, the trunks and branches of bare trees were heavy charcoal lines on a pale gray wall. Wrapped in white cloaks, the knights wandered through time, in a dreamlike region where people worshipped gods who had been gone from the western heart of Europe for hundreds of years. After riding for days through these trackless, hushed, nebulous forests, the knights all but forgot the nature of their journey, until, suddenly the white silence dropped into the screams of horses and dying children, and the snow was churned with charred earth and blood.

Every turning led toward death, while every urging of the human soul was toward life. This tension fascinated von Schnabelberg and became the basis of his faith. He had seen it in battle; men, women and children – soldiers or not – mortally wounded, unconscious and beyond help, offered last rites and given up for dead, could awaken to rejoin the world of human struggle. Others who seemed not so bad off would curdle into death without the blessing of God. Only God knew what would happen; only God knew the fate of a man.

Outside a burning village, von Schnabelberg had run with a terrified, wounded, barbarian girl in his arms. He brought her where she might be helped by the Order's doctor – or, where a priest could give her the Rite that she might at least pass out of this life into Heaven, vouchsafed a place by Christ.

"Get her out of here!" said a soldier. "We have little enough for ourselves!"

"She is innocent," said von Schnabelberg. "She is no enemy. She is dying. Could she not at least be given Christ's blessing now, at the end? She is so small. She need not have a bed. A fur on the ground is enough."

The priest looked up, hearing the sorrow in von Schnabelberg's voice. The battle had been ugly; though the town had not resisted much, that they resisted at all was enough to send the men into a frenzy of killing. As the priest watched the children in this village slaughtered, he thought of Herod and the Innocents and wondered if the important infant had been saved. Perhaps this girl was the Christ child. "Lay her here," he said, taking a wolf skin from the back of his chair and laying it on the floor of the tent. "She will be warm on this wolfskin. I will watch her."

"Thank you, Father."

The idea of mercy colored every other word of the litany of the Church. *Miserere, miserecordia, kyrie eleison*, and yet? Real mercy was rare. The girl soon slept. When morning came, von Schnabelberg returned to see if she had lived and found her sleeping, her thumb in her mouth. The priest had cleaned the deep arrow wound in her side and dressed it, wrapping bandages around her that could have been used for wounded soldiers. He looked up as von Schnabelberg entered.

"We never know," he said, simply. "The innocent we help might be the Lord himself. I believe she will live."

Though the territory they gained was bought in blood – their blood and that of those they conquered – there were many occasions when the people surrendered immediately, so von Schnabelberg had no cause to waver in his faith. He grew to hate war, its cruel horrors and unnecessary death, but he had seen enough of pagan rituals to remain convinced that Christ would bring peace and comfort to the people who embraced His offer of salvation.

He returned to his father's castle and married the girl his parents had chosen. He retained his position in the Order of Teutonic Knights, but he never again sought to serve the Cross on a crusade. He lived an idealistic, peaceful life in the midst of the constant power struggles and feuds all around him. The smallest shred of earth could be a force for goodness; this he believed, and he struggled to bring justice to everything he did. He became a beloved leader to the knights serving him. To help maintain and enforce peace, he donated land for a community of Knights Hospitaller. He was a generous landlord to those serving beneath him, men such as Lunkhofen, who had seen their own share of horror in battle. Von Schnabelberg regarded a life spent in the pursuit of the realization of Christian ideals as a life spent in the service of God, honoring his vows. No more could be demanded of a man. Now, watching the preparations of Conrad and Rudolf, he thought of his childless castle, and the dazzling resolution of Lunkhofen's glorious boys. The call of the Black Robes had touched him, too, reminding him of his youth.

***

The ceremony of investment was to be held in the cloister church of the Engelberg Monastery. All the nobles within a two-day ride of Apple Tree Village and people from Zürich, Luzern, Zug and Bremgarten were expected to be present for the ceremony and the feast afterward at Castle Lunkhofen. Von Schnabelberg had sponsored Conrad. Gretchen's father stood as Rudolf's sponsor, to show that his daughter had not been thrown over by young Lunkhofen but that, perhaps, she had withdrawn herself as her sacrifice for the Holy Crusade.

***

To Father Markus, Conrad confessed to impure thoughts, lying, anger at his father and mother, to a generalized lack of patience and non-attendance at Mass. For Conrad this was just a necessary preliminary to the real thing; the moment he was dubbed knight, his life would be consecrated to the great adventure. He had watched his mother embroider the black cross of the Teutonic Knight on his cape and felt a great surge of pride – which he confessed, also – and excitement at the prospect ahead of him. His heart beat, "Let me GO!"

This was one of the last steps, and the great one, the one in which the whole world would know that he was a knight in service to the Cross. Conrad was becoming the hero of his own romance, the man of whom the minnesingers sang.

Rudolf's confession was quite a different thing. In turning away from Gretchen, he felt he was turning toward his fate, to open combat with Satan. To win, he needed absolute concentration. To kill was clearly evil; to kill for Christ – to kill the enemies of Christ – was not.

Rudolf had never yearned for battle, nor had he wanted to join the tournaments his brother loved. The possibility of killing another made the mock war loved by noble youths impossible for him. To kill another just on a whim, for the possession of a moment of triumph and recognition, or for some lady's favor in an idle moment was pride, and it was murder. Though the Pope's injunction had been increasingly disregarded, it remained weakly alive and was sometimes enforced. Jousting was covetousness and vanity. Conrad had ridden twice and emerged victorious each time. His "enemies" had not died; they had surrendered. Rudolf felt Conrad had been lucky. "How would you take it," he had asked his brother, "if your friend Walther were dead now because of a game you played this afternoon?"

"It is my risk as well as his," answered Conrad. "It is a level field, and on such field we find out who is the better rider, the better with the lance. That is all it is."

"It isn't the same as when we were children," continued Rudolf. "This is a real lance you carry." He knew his younger brother's physical strength. The lance, at its largest circumference, could not be spanned by two hands. It was heavy enough to unseat a fully armed knight riding full tilt on a powerful horse, and it was deadly. It was Conrad's preferred weapon, though he practiced with the broadsword until he was its master, too.

"It is well," said Conrad, "for us to know how we would stand up to battle."

St. Bernhard had determined that killing the infidel in the name of Christ to save the Holy Cross was not a violation of God's commandments; he had cited Matthew: "For whosoever will save his life shall lose it: and whosoever will lose his life for my sake shall find it."

Conrad wondered how his gentle, melancholy brother would ever become the militant servant of Christ he would have to be.

"Rudolf, if a man came at you, bent on taking your life or stealing from God what belongs to God, would you kill then?"

"I would have to, Conrad," said Rudolf quietly. "It is what I have resolved to do, but there are more bitter enemies than those who would take my life, and not every field of battle is level."

***

Rudolf's confession was a painful labor for Father Markus, a simple man who followed God and the tenets of his faith with peaceful complacency. He yearned to quiet Rudolf with some simple platitudes and his own solid evaluation that there was little wrong with a normal young man that could not be cured by marriage and children.

"My son," he said when Rudolf paused, "perhaps it is that you take your own life too seriously and in thinking of yourself forget other people."

Rudolf heard this, not as it was meant, but as proof of his own emptiness, of the devil blinding him to the needs of others. Selfishness, nothing else, a vain fixation with himself.

"You are right, Father. I have hurt everyone. My father, my mother and the girl I was to marry. They do not seem to feel what I feel, that things are not the way they seem to be. All I do is hurt others," Rudolf's voice caught in his throat.

"Everyone is sad, Rudolf. It is the nature of human life; it is our fate to lose and to feel the loss, to doubt ourselves, to compare ourselves to others. For this God has given us the commandments. We can rouse our will against the darkness of sin through simple obedience."

Rudolf knelt in silence for a few minutes, then said, "I cannot find God anywhere, Father. I tell you the truth."

"You must pray; have faith that God will find you. He will not let you go if you but turn to Him."

"I turn to Him constantly, Father, and I find nothing there. With this emptiness inside of me, how can I take Mass in the morning?"

"Confess your sins to me, Rudolf. It is all you can do. I will intercede for you and ask for God's forgiveness. He never refuses this; think of the murderer on the cross beside that of our Lord. Incorrigible and yet, at the last moment, he turned to Christ and begged forgiveness. It was granted instantly. You will be forgiven, too, if you only ask."

"How can I ask forgiveness of a God I cannot be certain of?"

"How are you not certain, Rudolf? You are here now. Why are you going on Crusade? What has called you to this?"

"I am going to save myself from sin, Father. I am going for the Kingdom of Heaven and perhaps, on the way, I will find Him, but in any case, the Pope has said that the sins of those who go and fight for the cross will be forgiven. That is all I want, Father. I want forgiveness; I want to feel the Devil let go of my heart. I am afraid, Father, of the sins I do not know."

"God sees your heart, young lord. He knows you are repentant, even of what you cannot see."

"Is it enough, Father? How can I know I am forgiven?"

Father Markus sat in silence a moment. Here was the sin that Rudolf could not see. It was doubt. Faith was a thing of complete confidence; trust without question. "Have faith in God, Rudolf. Remember the mustard seed? The Kingdom of God is like the mustard seed, so small it cannot be seen and so large it fills the universe."

Rudolf nodded.

"Strive toward that, young lord. Pray for the simple faith of the mustard seed. And now, in the name of the Father, the Son and the Holy Spirit, I absolve you of your sins. Go, my child, prepare for your vigil and have no more of this morbid doubt."

"Ah," thought Father Markus, never a complicated man. "Rudolf is going that he might recover from a broken heart. Ah, that must be it. Little Gretchen has refused him. Many take the cross for such reasons." This was the conclusion the two fathers hoped that outsiders would reach on their own about the matter. A man thrown over by a girl was none the worse for it; a girl thrown over by a man was another thing completely.

Chapter 8, Vigil

Their new weapons and the mail they would wear in battle were placed before the altar. Conrad and Rudolf knelt on the stone floor, both in the clothing of their old lives, soon to be shed for the costumes of the Teutonic Knight. "Our Father who art in Heaven," said Conrad, kneeling some distance apart from Rudolf, fulfilling his vigil in this way. "What do I do in there all night?" he had asked Father Markus.

"Think on Christ's sufferings," answered the priest.

"All *NIGHT?*" Conrad wondered to himself, then asked again, "Yes, Father, but what do I DO?"

"Repeat 'Our Father' until you know that it is God's will to which you are subject, not your own."

"Meditate on this," Father Markus had told Rudolf, motioning toward the hanging statue, "and you will find your suffering is nothing in comparison." And so, as he knelt, Rudolf turned his eyes there. For a few moments, the moonlight threw the form of Christ crucified into a hard silhouette. During the years when his father was away, his mother, too, had spent hours in meditation of Christ's suffering. "Is my suffering anything compared to His?" she sincerely asked herself, and then wondered what agonies Heinrich might be enduring for the sake of this crucified man. Stricken with guilt for thinking of her own suffering rather than those of Christ, she began again.

Holding her infant son in one arm, the Holy Virgin kept vigil in the darkness with Rudolf and Conrad, her right hand raised in blessing.

When Rudolf was a child, he had wondered over and over why God had not consoled Anna in her loneliness. She prayed several times a day for Heinrich's return or, at the very least, some news. At first, Rudolf had leapt from bed each morning and run down to the hall believing the prayers of his mother would have brought his father home. The hall remained empty, and Anna's day began as had the one before it and the one before that, an endless chain of disappointment. The mystery to Rudolf was that Anna's days remained the same even after Heinrich returned; she had become one with misery.

"No," Rudolf thought to himself. "Don't think of that. Think of Him. What He endured for mankind." He turned his eyes from the Virgin Mother to the figure hung across the vault above the altar. The Savior faced toward the right, his eyes closed, his brow strung with rivulets of blood. His emaciated body twisted to one side; His skin pulled bluish across His ribs and hips. His feet were too large, broken and bleeding, beneath the nail that held them to the Cross. For more than a century, the Catholic world had been mobilized to avenge this man's death. "It is for my salvation He is there," thought Rudolf. "It is for me He suffered and died."

The man on the cross seemed to have surrendered to His agony.

"Could you have felt relieved?" he whispered. "All your dread, fulfilled in this moment? That's what I'm searching for," he prayed, "for relief, the moment I finally KNOW."

"It is not yours to know," the dark church echoed.

A shiver ran through Rudolf. Were these his thoughts echoing between the stone walls, or was God speaking to him, answering his questions?

"Lord?" he spoke in a low voice.

The candles flickered in a passing draft. The room was silent except for Conrad's mumbled prayers drifting at times into soft snores.

Rudolf thought again of the crucified Christ, of the events leading to His death, of the nights he spent trying to accept His Father's will for him. There had been a night like this. Christ was alone, in the desert, terrified, as Rudolf was terrified.

"Is this what I must be?" Rudolf wondered. "Had Christ

thought this? For Conrad things are clear and light; he thinks, he sees, he acts, all in concert, one will, his will, God's or his own? For Conrad, it is all one."

"You are not he." Again.

The room was silent.

"My mind?" asked Rudolf. "Or the tempter? I cannot tell. I can go to Jerusalem; I can remain here. It will not matter. God? There is nothing where God is supposed to be, nothing at all." He was suddenly seized by a wave of intense nausea. He bent forward, holding his hands against his cramping belly. "Forgive me, Lord, my thoughts are sinful." He breathed deeply and straightened, eyes fixed on the hanging man above him. *This pain is nothing*, he thought, *nothing compared to that pain*. The wound on Christ's side drew his attention. How much had they done to this man? He would have died just hanging on the cross, true, but such a death would have been slow torture. Perversely, the wounds He bore, and for which He was pitied, took Him more quickly to His Father and saved Him agonies. Was this kindness? Were the Roman soldiers kind to Christ to thrust their swords into Him this way? The blood painted on Christ's side was ever-fresh red. His bluish skin was the skin of death; this Christ was dead while the Christ in Mary's arms was as new as a spring wildflower and more rare.

"That is our life, Holy Father, that is the life of man. We are that babe and then life takes us and twists us and hangs us there and all around us wonder why this is so, and He, hanging there, reminds us of this constantly. We are fettered by the knowledge of our own death." Rudolf felt his face flush, heat from a kind of anger rushing from his pounding heart to his face. "And there is more. Below Him are his mother and His beloved friends. They wait for His body that they may wash it and place it where the animals cannot get at it, preserving it, as the home of His soul, the place where their hearts rest. That is what we do, God. Our hearts entwine around the hearts of others."

His mother had told him of his brothers born dead, never to see the light of day or the shadows of leaves on the walls. She always talked as if she had known them, as if they had been living, breathing boys. Rudolf felt that somehow God had cheated the family, that his mother might have found happiness had these two small children lived. He felt, always, that he was a consolation prize, the third, not the firstborn son. Could he live up to what they might have been? "That woman," he said, looking at the statue of the Virgin Mary, "lost her child, God, all for you."

"Not for me. For you."

Rudolf heard the words, and for a moment felt their weight. "For me," he thought. "For me?"

"For your life, your everlasting life."

"That is it," moaned Rudolf, "what I cannot believe. That is Satan's handhold!" Again his belly cramped, this time with such force that he fell to the floor, calling out in pain.

"Rudolf!" Conrad called back. "What has happened?" He went to his brother, who lay crying on the stones while holding his stomach. Conrad knelt beside his brother, taking his hand. At his touch, Rudolf relaxed on the stone floor. Conrad lifted his brother's head and held it against his own chest. "Brother, you are ill," he said.

"No," said Rudolf, his voice hoarse and breathy. "I am afraid."

Chapter 9, Vows

We fight for the honor of the most glorious Virgin,
The mother of our Lord Jesus Christ,
For the honor and defense of the Holy Church
And for all the Christian faith
And for the expulsion of the enemies of the Cross
Gott mit uns!

Oath of the Teutonic Knights

At daybreak, Father Markus found the brothers kneeling side-by-side, hand-in-hand. "Come," he said. "You will now bathe and prepare for Mass."

The bath was symbolic of a new baptism, new vows, a new, more serious life and a new social status as warriors for Christ and pilgrims of the Holy Cross. They would dress in white undergarments and above these would be placed the surcoat and cloak of the Teutonic Knight embroidered with the black crosses of their Order. Rudolf's had been made by Gretchen and her mother. The surcoat carried an embroidered image of the Schneebeli coat of arms — three snowballs on a red ground — letting all know that Rudolf rode for Sir Adelbert, redeeming not only his own sins and those of his sponsor, but also those of his wife and daughter through their work. The stitching was neat and small though Gretchen's eyes had been blinded by tears. Gretchen's mother felt it unfair, but Sir Adelbert insisted that without this tribute, it would look as if Rudolf had spurned Gretchen. "This must not be the world's view," he told his wife, "or it will go harder yet for our daughter. She's well out of it. She will realize that before long, believe me."

Gretchen's mother knew this. When Rudolf had left, she hoped time would work on Gretchen's young heart and another love would come to fill it.

Anna had made Conrad's clothing, and his surcoat bore his

family coat of arms neatly embroidered between two arms of the cross. His shield would bear the castle crest of the house of Schnabelberg. Anna had made Heinrich's cloak and surcoat, too, when she was carrying Conrad. It was a cruel, dim punishment to repeat this all for her golden son. Her stitches were stitches of sorrow mixed with rage; her heart, like Gretchen's heart, was broken, but there was little chance of it being filled someday by a love that equaled this. Her heart was such that it ran toward what was absent and away from what was near.

"How could you let them go?" she had asked Heinrich over and over again.

"I cannot stop them, Anna. I would. I would stop all of them." He then stormed out of the castle to the stable, where he found Conrad. "You have sent me to Hell, my boy, to Hell," he said, and banged his fist against a pole.

"Father, I am sorry."

"Sorry. You will be dead. That is your 'sorry.' Your romantic foolishness has broken your mother's heart and now? I will be left with nothing. All of this and for whom?"

"I will be back."

"God-willing. God is seldom willing. Of those who went with us not even one in five returned. Why do you think there is this endless call? It is because men die."

Heinrich was exhausted with all of it, with Anna's unending sorrow, with his sons' blindness, with the calls of one Pope after another. As he dressed for that morning's ceremony, to be followed by a banquet at the castle for which his wife had been preparing for weeks, he saw no justice in any of it. He had gone. That should be enough. That this land had come to his father through the death of others was meager consolation. But the Crusades continued from generation to generation, and as things were, Heinrich must publicly show pride in his sons, for their courage, for their faith and for the sacred honor they would bestow upon his empty castle by fighting for the Holy Cross.

"Damn them!" he muttered under his breath and quickly crossed himself. "Lord God, forgive me. Please do something to stop at least one of them from going. It matters little which."

He found Anna in her chamber, seated before a polished mirror, braiding her hair with the help of a young girl servant. "We must go, Anna."

She looked up at him reflected in her mirror. Her mouth was set in a hard, pink line. Heinrich knew it would remain that way for a very long time.

***

Dressed as Teutonic Knights, Sir Adelbert and Duke von Schnabelberg came into the room where the brothers were bathing. They carried the clothes the brothers would wear that day; the garments were white, symbolizing their rebirth and the purity of their hearts. After they had dressed, they returned to the sanctuary and knelt before the altar, with their sponsors beside them.

Father Markus entered, and all rose. Rudolf looked around him at the room where he had spent such a strange and terrible night. It seemed quite ordinary now; the vessels for the Mass were set out on the altar, gleaming gold and silver in the candlelight. Anna stood beside Gretchen and her mother. Gretchen's red-rimmed eyes filled with tears of rage now more than sorrow. In her mind ran the beautiful love songs the minnesinger had sung the rainy day that now seemed so long ago:

> *On such a cloud of joy as this,*
> *My soul has never sailed so high before.*
> *I hover as on wings of bliss,*
> *With thoughts of only her, whom I adore,*
> *Because her love unlocked the door,*
> *Which leads into my inmost heart?*
> *And entered there for evermore.*

He had looked into her eyes as if they held the whole world.

How could that man have brought this with him, too? Gretchen could not understand. "Evermore," had proven brief. The rain-sogged springtime had been the most beautiful world anyone had known. She had lived in Rudolf's love, and when she slipped into sleep at night, the memory of his loving eyes lay behind her closed lids. She closed her eyes for a moment to see if she could find them still, but they were no longer there.

It is bad enough that you would leave me, she thought, as she gazed at the kneeling form in front of the church, *but that you would die as well?* She thought of a world in which Rudolf were completely absent. *Will it be easier to bear if you are killed?* Her heart shuddered unevenly inside her. *Holy Mary*, she prayed suddenly, silently, *ask the forgiveness of our Heavenly Father for me, for I have wished Rudolf dead.* She crossed herself quickly; her mother, noticing the gesture, reached for her daughter's hand. She would have spared her daughter this. She knew the sweet, confiding, open and loving girl would never be the same. Gretchen would hesitate to give her love. In the future, she would keep part to herself.

"We must find a match for her quickly," she had told her husband. "When she has a child, she will again know love."

She turned and looked at Anna on the other side of her. She noted the hard straight line of Anna's mouth and the bitter compression in the corners of her eyes. *Not Gretchen*, she thought fiercely. *I will not have that for her.*

Father Markus sang, "*Asperges me.*"

The choir of monks answered, "*Domine, hyssopo, et mundabor: lavabis me, et super nivem dealbabor. Misere mei, Deus, secundum magnam misericordiam tuam.*"

"*Gloria Patri, et Filio, et Spiritu Sancto,*" said Father Markus as he made the sign of the cross over the four kneeling before him, sprinkling them with holy water dropped from the branches of the hyssop, as written in the psalm. They were cleansed of all evil that clung to them, purified by God's great, merciful love.

"*Sicut erat in principio, et nunc, et semper, et in saecula saeculorum*," responded the people in the sanctuary, singing, then, "Amen."

When the time came for the reading of the psalm, Conrad and Rudolf knew that the most serious moment neared. It was the psalm traditional to pilgrimage. It was the first of their vows. For them, Jerusalem was to be a place of landscape, not only of heart; no longer the faraway sacred town where Christ was judged, but the City of God they hoped to re-conquer and return to those to whom it belonged. "Psalm 115," said Father Markus, picking up his psalter, though he knew the psalm by heart – as did many of those in the church that morning.

"I have believed, therefore have I spoken; but I have been humbled exceedingly."

"I said in my excess: Every man is a liar," responded the people.

"What shall I render to the Lord, for all the things He hath rendered unto me?"

"I will take the chalice of salvation; and I will call upon the name of the Lord."

"I will pay my vows to the Lord before all His people," said Father Markus.

"…precious in the sight of the Lord is the death of His saints," the congregation replied.

Anna had fire in her eyes. Heinrich could feel this even though she was across the church, distant from him, in the women's section.

"O Lord, for I am thy servant: I am thy servant, and the son of thy handmaid. Thou hast broken my bonds."

"I will sacrifice to thee the sacrifice of praise, and I will call upon the name of the Lord."

Praise? No. These sons of my friend, washed and dressed up there. Lambs for the slaughter, thought Mayor Mülner. *Virgin sheep, ready for the knife.* His fists clenched beside the hem of his surcoat; he, too, wore a costume that told all his history and his vows; he was dressed as a sergeant of the Teutonic Order.

"I will pay my vows to the Lord in the sight of all His people."

"In the courts of the house of the Lord, in the midst of thee, O Jerusalem."

Jerusalem! thought Conrad. *Indeed, I shall be in Jerusalem!* His heart soared as if it might break free.

"*In nomini Patrii, Figlii, e Spiritu Sanctu*, Amen."

Rudolf knelt in a trance, carried on the flood of ritual, the expectation of rites. He had little to do; his thinking of the night before had left him exhausted and confused. He could feel the presence of his parents, watching their sons take this enormous step away from them.

Anna would keep all she loved near where she could reach for them at any moment to reassure her of their presence, their being. Rudolf was certain his mother never completely believed that Heinrich was at Castle Lunkhofen, beside her. Their relationship was strained – all knew this – and her anger never fully faded because it came from fear. Rudolf knew this from all the nights he had spent with her in prayer for the return of Heinrich; she prayed with the hope – but without the belief – that her prayers would bring him back to her. Her prayers and her readings were incantations, bargains. "Anything, Heavenly Father, anything, if only you return my Heinrich safely to me." Heinrich was her real god.

Perhaps God had come to collect His due. It was nothing more than He had asked of Abraham, nothing more than He had offered up Himself.

This is God's justice? thought Rudolf for a moment in complete wonderment.

***

After all had shared the body and blood of Christ, the service turned to the knighting of Conrad.

"Who comes forth to sponsor Conrad as he assumes the duties of knighthood? Who will confer upon him the honor? Who will gird his sword?"

Von Schnabelberg came forward to stand before the priest who held out the silver-covered gospel. "Place upon our Lord's holy word your right hand," he said, and when von Schnabelberg had done this, the priest continued, saying, "Do you vow that you are a free man of noble birth, of fitting station to make this boy a knight?"

"I so vow, Father."

"Do you here vow to instruct this young knight in the duties and austerities of knighthood?"

"I so vow, Father."

"In the name of the Father, the Son and the Holy Spirit," said the priest, sprinkling von Schnabelberg with holy water, "you may proceed."

Duke von Schnabelberg turned toward the altar, knelt, and prayed that he might have God's blessing in dubbing Conrad. He then stood and, bending down, lifted Conrad's new sword from the floor in front of the altar. He turned to the priest. In both hands, he held the sword out towards the priest, the hilt upright, the blade pointed at the ground.

"Father, I beg your blessing on this sword, which goes with Conrad into battle, the symbol to him always of the vows he takes today and his duties to uphold, protect and serve the Holy Cross in all parts of the world."

The priest made the sign of the cross over the sword and said, "Lord, bless this sword that is dedicated to your service."

Conrad knelt still, facing the altar. Von Schnabelberg came to him. "Stand, Conrad, that I may gird on your sword."

Conrad's heart pounded. The moment he had longed for was near. He felt a great joy rise inside him as he stood. It would happen after all, adventure and the world. He could imagine himself and his black horse riding across the wild and empty territories of the infidel. He stood, head bowed, heart thrilled before von Schnabelberg.

"With the girding of this sword, I confer upon you the duties and obligations of knighthood. Do you vow, Conrad, to serve God and the Holy Virgin with all your heart?"

"I so vow."

"Do you, Conrad, vow to keep the Ten Holy Commandments and the Seven Holy Sacraments at all times, wherever you may be?"

"I so vow."

"Do you vow to fight for the Holy Cross wherever you find it is maligned, protecting the true faith against her enemies?"

"I so vow."

"Do you vow to come to the aid of those who are less fortunate, to offer help to the poor, succor to the sick, and kindness to those who suffer?"

"I so vow."

"Do you vow faith to your earthly lord, to provide aid in times of distress, leaving behind your own concerns?"

"I so vow."

"Then I now gird upon you your own sword. Do you vow to use this sword only in service to God, never in wanton jousting, never in a duel against a brother, never in any cause but that to which you have sworn yourself. Do you so vow?"

"I so vow."

The duke wrapped the belt around Conrad's slim waist and buckled it; the sword hung in the sheath to the side.

"Kneel, Conrad, that I may confer upon you the status of knight."

Conrad knelt before von Schnabelberg, who then lifted his right hand and delivered a hard blow to Conrad's neck. It was finished.

Sir Adelbert and Heinrich came forward. As Rudolf and Conrad took their vows, they, with von Schnabelberg, would renew theirs. Heinrich sending his sons to the Holy Land was a sacrifice the church recognized as an act of penance by Heinrich himself. Sir Adelbert, as Rudolf's sponsor in knighthood, would stand beside Rudolf at this moment. Then, von Schnabelberg, to the surprise of all, himself took the cross. He would go with Conrad and Rudolf.

The priest held out to them the gospel. Piling their hands on the Bible's silver cover, they vowed to take the Cross to Jerusalem, to pray at the church of the Holy Sepulcher and to fight the infidel until the Holy City was returned to the followers of the true faith. It was a vow to use war as pilgrimage and prayer.

"You have vowed before Heaven and all here to take the symbol of our faith and Christ's suffering to those who deny it, who, emboldened by the tempter, choose to live in heresy and sin. Do not forget this. They choose and in so choosing, they choose their own death, not in this world alone, but death in the world everlasting."

"Remember that the Knights of Christ may safely fight the battles of their Lord. Lest on the battlefield you feel remorse, that perhaps you sin in killing the infidel, I admonish you now in the words of the blessed St. Bernhard, 'Go forth confidently, you knights, and with a stalwart heart, repel the foes of the cross of Christ. Not death nor life can separate you from the love of God which is in Jesus Christ, and in every peril repeat, 'Whether we live or whether we die, we are the Lord's.' What a glory to return in victory from such a battle! How blessed to die there as a martyr! Rejoice if you live and conquer in the Lord; but exult even more if you die and join your Lord. Life indeed is a fruitful thing and victory is glorious, but a holy death is more important than either. If they are blessed who die in the Lord, how much more are they who die for the Lord!'"

"May the Lord be with you!"

"And with your spirit," answered the people standing.

"Go, you are sent forth."

"Thanks be to God."

"May the tribute of my worship be pleasing to You, most Holy Trinity, and grant that the sacrifice which I, though unworthy, have offered may be acceptable to You, and through Your mercy obtain forgiveness for me and all for whom I have offered it. Through Christ our Lord. Amen."

"May Almighty God bless you, in the name of the Father, and the Son, and the Holy Spirit."

"Amen."

It was over. Conrad was knighted. Rudolf, knighted a year

earlier after his service to Adelbert, was set upon his course of salvation.

When Rudolf and Conrad rode away from Castle Lunkhofen, they rode behind Duke von Schnabelberg as their Commander. Others joined them. When they reached Venice, they were a force of knights, servants and sergeants, numbering in all more than 300 men. They boarded ships bound for the headquarters of the Teutonic Knights in Acre.

Book Two: Blood

Chapter 10, Acre

"It is therefore with the desire for peace that wars are waged, even by those who take pleasure in exercising their warlike nature in command and battle. And hence it is obvious that peace is the end sought for by war. For every man seeks peace by waging war, but no man seeks war by making peace." St. Augustine, *The City of God*

The three hundred -- knights, sergeants, foot soldiers and servants -- were admitted to the hospice of the Teutonic Order in Acre by a one-eyed sergeant who, after giving them God's blessing, told them to wait. Their ranks filled the hall.

A young priest rushed in to greet them. "We heard you were coming. Come along. Let me take you to the dormitory. You and your men must be tired from the journey."

"We would not displace anyone," replied von Schnabelberg.

The priest looked up at him confused and quickly shook his head. "You will displace no one," he said. Looking into his eyes, von Schnabelberg saw sorrow with no bottom. It was indeed as they had heard in Venice.

"At vespers I will come back to take you to Mass," the priest told him. "After is our dinner and you will meet the prior. He would have you and your men rest first."

They followed him down a long corridor and turned into the large dormitory, lined with narrow beds. Tables down the middle, flanked by chairs, served as desks for writing.

"Thank you, Father."

When the priest had left, the young knights looked from one to the other. The stillness of the city had bewildered them. Though markets were open and people went about their business in a regular way – or so it seemed – dread and sorrow overhung everything. The dormitory, empty even of the possessions of men, bewildered them further. "I fear," said von Schnabelberg to all of them, "that we have heard the truth on our journey."

"Then we've come too late!" said Conrad. He turned to the wall and hit it with his fist. "If the ships had been ready!"

"Ah, Conrad. You do not know. It is God's will," said von Schnabelberg, "that we arrive now, so the time is perfect. We will do what is asked of us."

***

The prior had come to Acre as a young monk when he had found his soul too restless and his faith too hot for him to remain in the monastic cloister. Believing that no man could live in peace without the salvation offered by Jesus Christ, he had followed the Emperor and the Grand Master, Hermann von Salza some dozen years before. He had seen so much -- the coronation of Fredrick II as King of Jerusalem, the negotiated, precious peace, the expansion of the hospital in Jerusalem, the replenishment of the headquarters in Acre where he lived, the rebuilding and fortification of the stone castle, Starkenberg.

The fall of Jerusalem had broken his heart and filled him with doubt. He had followed the knights on the familiar road to Jerusalem and into that slaughter, where hundreds upon hundreds fell until most of those he'd come to serve were dead. *"Gott mit uns"*? No. Where had God been? He had watched them fall and could give them nothing. That their souls were safe with God suddenly did not matter.

He returned to Acre with the few survivors and continued his duties with a gaping hole in his own faith, with faint hope that the forms he practiced would lead him back to the spirit, for the sake of the ritual itself -- and because he knew no other life.

He entered the chapel and saw the hundred or so knights already kneeling on the stone floor, heads bowed. Here was all the regimentation in which he had found comfort, the cleanliness of their capes, their fresh faces. The censer swung in arcs across the nave; the sweet smoke cleansed the air and prepared the way for the entrance of the Lord. *"In nominee Patris, et Filii, et Spiritu sancti, Amen,"* said the prior, facing the crucifix hanging behind the altar in the front of the chapel.

He offered his confession, asking those who knelt behind him for their blessing and forgiveness. In one voice they answered, "May almighty God have mercy on you, forgive you all your sins, and bring you to everlasting life."

A tiny light flickered in the prior's heart. It was hope. He squirmed because he knew that hope's companion was misery. He knew where these boys were going and shuddered at the hopelessness of their journey. They then confessed to him, all in one voice, their Latin inflected with German.

"May Almighty God have mercy on you, forgive you your sins, and bring you to everlasting life," answered the prior.

"May the Almighty and Merciful Lord grant us pardon, absolution, and remission of our sins." As one, the small army crossed itself.

"Show us, Lord, Your mercy."

"And grant us Your salvation."

"O Lord, hear my prayer."

"And let my cry come unto You."

The prior moved forward to the altar, knelt, and kissed it. His inaudible prayer asked the Lord to take from all of them the evil within them. Rudolf knew these words; how often had he knelt on the stones of the chapel at Lunkhofen, his head resting on the small altar, saying them over and over again? "Take away from me my iniquity that I can come near the Holy of Holies."

The altar held a fragment of the True Cross. A simple, homely splinter of wood within a crystal globe, it rested in a small cup of hammered silver rimmed in gold beneath a tiny spire from which the angel Gabriel blew the trumpet of the Day of Judgment. "By the True Cross, a piece of which lies within our altar, give us your mercy and pardon our sins."

The prior stood and lifted the censer. The fragrance of the burning incense purified the air around the altar as if it were the hand of God brushing away the sins of mankind. He sang, then, "*Kyrie eleison*," and the young knights and their leader responded in kind, asking for God's mercy.

Rudolf stood, responded, knelt and prayed as he had all his life. The form held him to his past, but unlike the prior, Rudolf found no ease or hope in the ritual. After all, here he was again, face-to-face with the same knowledge that within him was something unspeakable. His heart pounded. His face burned in a rush of anxiety, and he desperately wanted out, or, rather, Satan wanted out. Satan could not bear the sight of the cross or endure the Holy Word so he created this terrible fear in Rudolf so he would stand up and leave. Rather than pulling away from him on this long journey, Rudolf felt Satan drawing closer and closer to the core of his heart, scratching the surface of his soul.

How could he take Holy Communion? He was polluted, evil. But what would he say if someone asked him – and someone would, his brother if no one else – why he refused the sacrament? He could say that during the Mass he'd been distracted by lustful thoughts of a girl he had seen on the street. He would lie. Sin piled on sin in Satan's intricate net.

"May the Lord be with you," said the prior.

"And with your Spirit," responded the men.

"Let us pray," said the prior.

Rudolf had never felt so far from God as he did in this chapel.

"That we are not alone on this earth is Your gift to us," said the prior. "You gave us Your Son that we might not fear death. *In nomini Patris, Fillis, et Spiritu Sanctus*, Amen."

The men stood. The young priest serving the prior began Psalm 79:1-5. "Oh God, the heathen are come into thine inheritance; thy holy temple have they defiled; they have laid Jerusalem into heaps."

The knights responded, "The dead bodies of thy servants have they given to be meat unto the fowls of heaven, the flesh of thy saints unto the beasts of the earth."

"Their blood have they shed like water round about Jerusalem; and there was none to bury them."

"How long, Lord? Wilt Thou be angry forever?"

"The Word of God," said the priest.

"May we be worthy," responded the men.

"I will read to you from Numbers, God giving instructions to Moses on his entry to the Promised land. 'And the Lord spake unto Moses in the plains of Moab by Jordan, near Jericho, saying, *"Speak unto the children of Israel, and say unto them, When ye are passed over Jordan into the land of Canaan, then ye shall drive out all the inhabitants of the land from before you, and destroy all their pictures, and destroy all their molten images and quite pluck down all their high places; And ye shall dispossess the inhabitants of the land and dwell therein: for I have given you the land to possess it... But if you will not drive out the inhabitants of the land from before you, then it shall come to pass that those which ye let remain of them shall be pricks in your eyes, and thorns in your sides, and shall vex you in the land wherein ye dwell. Moreover, it shall come to pass that I shall do unto you as I thought to do unto them."*

"The Word of God."

"Thanks be to God," said the men.

The priest then prayed, "Cleanse my heart and my lips, O Almighty God, Who cleansed the lips of the Prophet Isaiah with a burning coal. In Your gracious mercy, deign so to purify me that I may worthily proclaim Your holy Gospel. Through Christ our Lord. Amen."

The prior responded, "The Lord be in your heart and on your lips that you may worthily and fittingly proclaim His holy Gospel. In the name of the Father, and of the Son and of the Holy Spirit."

"May the Lord be with you," responded the priest.

"And with your Spirit," spoke the men again as one.

The silver and jeweled covers of the Holy Gospel gleamed in

the candlelight as the prior lifted it from the Altar and removed its silken cover. "I will read from the Book of the Blessed Saint Luke, Chapter 21, verses nine through twenty-five. *'Nation shall rise against nation, and kingdom against kingdom…and some of you shall they cause to be put to death…and when ye shall see Jerusalem compassed with armies then know that the desolation thereof is nigh, then let them which are in Judea flee to the mountains, and let them which are in the midst of it depart out; and let not them that are in the countries enter thereinto. For these are the days of vengeance, that all things which are written may be fulfilled…for there shall be great distress in the land and wrath upon this people and they shall fall by the edge of the sword, and shall be led a*way captive into all nations; and Jerusalem shall be trodden down.' Praise to you, O Christ!"

The priest responded, "May the words of the gospel wipe away our sins!"

Facing the men, the prior began the homily, explicating all the images of destruction and the absence of God. Never in his life had Rudolf heard anything quite like this. Behind the common forms and terms invoking God's aid, Christ's blessing, and the Holy Spirit's presence, was a brutal despair. It made sense to Rudolf that a man's sins would be wiped out by this Gospel of annihilation and loss. That was exactly why he was where he was. It justified the gruesome work for which he had been training with an intensity that approached obsession. Rudolf hoped that in lifting the sword of death against the infidel, he would meet his own death while in this blessed state of absolution. He was terrified by the depth of his yearning for it. What opened before him at this moment was not God's glorious grace, but the emptiness of the pit of Hell. He could not wait to fight.

"Nothing in God's world happens without cause. God was clear with Moses in telling him, 'Ye shall dispossess the inhabitants of the land and dwell therein.' Would God tell us anything different today? We men of Christ have lived in this holy land now more than six generations. Is it any wonder we have lost Jerusalem? To suit our convenience and desire for wealth, we have allowed the infidel to remain. The Lord God has said that such as those '...shall be thorns in our sides', and if we do not drive them out, He, the Lord God will do to us what He would have had us to do them. As God promised, '...there shall be great distress in the land and wrath upon the people and they shall fall by the edge of the sword, and shall be led away captive into all nations; and Jerusalem shall be trodden down.' What is there for us to do now? Is it too late for us?"

Rudolf shared in the body and blood of Christ with a pounding heart and the conviction that he had no right; he did this so as not to be known by the others, to conceal the great emptiness inside. No one would have believed the lie he had concocted, and it seemed too much to add sin to sin.

***

The tables in the refectory were covered in white linen. The resident monks served the men a good meal of meat and bread and fruit. It was not a usual meal; it was in honor of their arrival and in recognition of their need. They ate in silence, as their vows required, and as they ate, a priest read from St. Augustine's *City of God*.

Once the meal was finished and the rule of silence lifted, the prior turned to von Schnabelberg. "My Lord Duke, I would speak with you frankly."

"Shall I dismiss these men?"

"They may remain if they wish; what I will tell you they must hear either from you later or from me now."

The prior's heart held an abyss where once was hope.

"What have you heard of how things have gone here?" asked the prior, willing to tell less than all, though he longed to tell all until his memory of events dulled through recitation.

"We heard stories in Venice. Hysterical rumors or truth, I do not know," answered von Schnabelberg.

"There are no Christians remaining in Jerusalem. A few have escaped to Gaza, but most are dead. The leaders of the orders? All dead."

"How?"

"It is a story that will show just how much these infidels lack God." The prior crossed himself, knowing he, too, was bereft of God. "Khwaresmians. Tribes from north of the Tigris and Euphrates. They were chased out of their country by the Mongols. They fight for one or the other Ayyubid Sultans who use them to fight against each other. A few months ago, they stormed through the valley of the Jordan, destroying everything. They burned many holy places. It was they who sacked Jerusalem. They and Mamluks, led by a young infidel, Baibars."

"Mamluks? These, too, we have heard of. Who are they?"

"Slaves. For generations they have been used by the infidel to fight us; they are fierce, captured mountain people from above Baghdad. And slaves they remain. Who knows how these boys are used by the men who buy them – and they? They were slaves themselves. In their lives, they learn only two things. They learn to kill, and they learn to pray to their false god. When they are old enough – and their potential for evil is fulfilled – they are set free. Their owner gives them a horse, weapons with which to fight, and armor that serves the infidel as protection. But what do they do once freed?"

"I have no idea, Father."

"In their depravity, they turn back, freed men, and offer their service to the man who enslaved them! Each one does the same. They do not fight as men; they are devils."

The duke shook his head in bewilderment. "They are mercenaries?"

"Not even. Devils," said the priest. "If you were to see them in battle you would believe that the forces of Satan were released on the earth and that the holy vision of St. John had come to pass. They ride toward our ranks, screaming 'Allah!' while making shrill horrible sounds with their tongues, calling on their false god to protect them, to bring them victory. Though they win a battle, they do not win the kingdom of Heaven. That much is sure. They are as likely to raid an infidel town as a Christian. They will kill their own people."

"Had no one sounded a warning of the attack on Jerusalem?"

"We had warning. All summer infidel armies – Khwaresmians again -- raided Christian settlements around Jerusalem. Entire villages, men, women, children – all." The prior crossed himself. "Bless their souls. They rest in Heaven, but to die so horribly? They were alive when these barbarians impaled them on tall poles and left them in the sun, lining the roads. We knew Jerusalem was their object. The raids gave grim warning. In August, the Christians of Jerusalem set out as refugees to Jaffa. No one tried to stop them." His deep sorrow was clear in his determined control over his voice. He spoke in precise syllables, as if his words came from the end of a quill.

Von Schnabelberg shook his head. The prior took a deep breath and went on.

"The refugees were not quite halfway to Jaffa. You can be sure that each moment of peace increased their dread and their hope equally. Jaffa would be certain safety, well fortified in front, backed against the sea. But to lose the Holy City? No one wanted that. We have done all we have known to keep it. These men and women had left their homes, but life…" the priest stopped, his voice caught on the word.

Von Schnabelberg waited. The prior took a deep breath and continued, "Riders on our horses, with our saddles and wearing our clothes, came to them. Some were dressed as Poor Brethren and, speaking French, told the refugees, 'Turn around! All is safe. Our standards fly over the city! The Sultan, as-Salih Ayyub, has promised us safety and peace, a truce, a treaty! Come back!'

That was exactly what all the refugees wanted. They did not ask any questions. God's innocents, they turned round, blinded by hope and great yearning, even by their faith in God. They returned and saw the flags flying above the Citadel. Have you been to Jerusalem?"

"No."

"A great pity," said the prior, crossing himself. "It's doubtful you will see it now."

"The refugees, rejoicing at the sight of the flags, entered confidently through David's Gate. All appeared to be unchanged. Their fervent hopes won over their reason, and they were blind to the infidel's devious evil."

"They were attacked immediately?"

"No. They returned to their homes. When they were settled and had returned to their daily lives, the infidel began to harass and attack them. This went on day after day; men, women and children were killed in the streets until such a terror was built into the people that they no longer knew what to do. Young men and women were kidnapped and enslaved. The people feared going out and soon were trapped in their homes without water and without food."

"Clearly the infidel is without God."

"They decided to fight back. Those who could not fight – the old people, children, nuns, those who were ill -- hid within the Church of the Holy Sepulcher and on the mount of Calvary – places holy to all. They believed they would be safe, but they were not. The infidel desecrated these most holy places, murdering the helpless, and adding their blood to the blood of our Savior."

"Where were the Military Orders? Did they not resist?"

"When it was known to them, yes. For two days there was fighting in the streets of Jerusalem, but in the end, it was lost. We were woefully outnumbered. Thousands died. Those who survived wish they hadn't."

"How many of the knights remain?"

"Fewer than 100. Walter de Brienne leads them."

"It is God's will, then, that we arrive now when we are most needed."

"Ha," said the prior. "You will make little difference against the numbers of the infidel. Tens of thousands of Khwaresmians, an entire people now without a home."

Von Schnabelberg shuddered at the thought. "So many?"

Conrad could no longer control himself. "Where are they? We will join them, for the glory, for the kingdom of God."

The prior answered Conrad, but spoke to von Schnabelberg. "They are at La Forbie, near Gaza. You will join them. Ride south. But," said the prior, "I shudder for your men. I fear you have little chance of surviving any battle against these demons."

"Father, is it not true that with God no army is lost?" Conrad asked.

The prior looked at the floor.

"Conrad!" reprimanded von Schnabelberg. With a clear idea what they might be riding toward, he would insist on obedience in everything. Only with obedience could they hope to make any headway against the infidel forces. They could not be what they were – impetuous, youthful, separate beings. They must become – and remain – a unified force against which the infidel could find no opening.

"You cannot be lost, my son," sighed the prior, speaking the necessary words. "You fight for God." The prior thought to himself that the kingdom of God would be vouchsafed to this boy if he were killed in battle; there was at least that. There had been a time, the prior recalled, when that had not seemed to him a small thing. "Excuse me," he said to von Schnabelberg and the others. "I must prepare for compline." He turned and walked with determined quick steps through the archway leading out of the refectory. His faith might, after all, be regained from the forms of worship. The prior was determined to try. Without this effort, he had nothing left.

Chapter 11, La Forbie
"Gott mit uns!"

They went in ships to Jaffa, then on horse south to La Forbie in a trance of religious ecstasy. They believed absolutely that they would regain Jerusalem. When they reached the camp, they saw an array of dirty tents ranged in short cordilleras on the exposed plain. Odors of tethered animals, offal, cooking and human sweat hung heavy in the muggy air. On the edges of the Christian camp were the tents of the Bedouin tribes following al-Mansur Ibrahim allied with them against the forces of al-Salih Ayyub. Only about two hundred Christian knights were camped upon the plain. The sad and battle-weary faces of the men who met them could have told them everything -- had the raw young knights been able to see.

The weary, brokenhearted leader of the Hospitaller forces looked at the young men thinking only that they had come to die. "Would there were more of you," he said softly. The blind courage of the uninitiated was a weapon the men waiting on the sea plain no longer had. Still, numbers mattered more.

Since the sack of Jerusalem, Walter de Brienne and his men had endured long, grim hours of torpid inertia camped here, their spirits heavier than their armor. Beneath their mail all wore thick wool felt tunics from neck to knee; these protected them from arrows. Beneath that, a shirt. Their legs were covered with woolen hose worn under the mail leggings, but as the days passed, each hotter than the one before, they shed layers of safety and wandered around the camp in shirt and hose. Who cared if a sniper's arrow picked them off? They were in Hell now. Death would bring Heaven.

The enemy Ayyubid forces, led by Baibars the Mamluk, out-numbered them by a factor of thousands. The Syrian allies were right in advising them that the best strategy would be to wait until

Baibars' twenty-thousand mercenary Khwaresmians got tired of waiting, abandoned their Ayyubid allies, and returned to the normal paths of their wandering, raiding existence.

Survivors of the sack of Jerusalem lived in the darkness of shame. To die for the holy city would have been glorious, but instead, there was this soul-sucking dullness. To redeem themselves for the crime of survival, they removed their shoes and walked barefoot on burning sand; beneath the heavy felt others strung knotted ropes that rubbed their chests and backs raw as they trained under the hot sun. Too many of the army wished to die for anyone to even hope for victory. The entire company was fasting and torturing itself into a state of wild desperation, while rumors spread that added fruitless anxiety to the misery of waiting.

Seeing this sad group, von Schnabelberg's young knights were even more convinced that they had been sent by God. *"Gott mit uns!"* became more than a prayer and battle cry. It was a statement of fact. God was with them, or they would not have arrived when they did. They sought every possible way to demonstrate to God the purity of their souls and their submission to His will. They renewed their vows of chastity, poverty and obedience so they could perform as God's chosen army. The rivalries which emerge naturally when men are close together receded in the face of a greater urgency, and men who had until now hated each other, trained as brothers. Those who had, in their journey, broken the vows of chastity, spent hours in prayer and seeking forgiveness, confessed and begged the priests for penance. These wandered in the dark of night murmuring "Our Father" in low voices until the number prescribed had been reached, and they were freed from the burden of their sin. Conrad was one of these.

Conrad had never imagined that his older brother would emerge the stronger knight; the more forceful, the more disciplined and directed toward the matter of killing, and Rudolf became the leader of a company. The gray warhorse, given him a world ago by Sir Adelbert, had become almost a part of his own body. Training was penance, and Rudolf, living always in the twilight of doubt, pushed himself, his horse, and his men; all obeyed his commands though the days were bitterly long and unbearably hot. At night, they threw themselves into the deep, dreamless sleep for which Rudolf yearned.

On a night soon after the autumnal equinox, Rudolf fell immediately into profound sleep and dreamed that they had gone to battle and it was over. He watched as the dead on the battlefield were lifted into the emptiness of the pale blue sky, reaching for the hand of God, their horses scattering across the world. He alone felt the pull of Satan, his relentless hand on his ankle, closing ever more tightly, holding him back, pulling him down. "Why?" Rudolf cried out to God in his sleep.

"You? No. Not you."

"But why?"

"You question me?"

"That is my sin. I question." He awoke, startled, shaking with chills, in the tent he shared with Conrad.

"Rudolf?" said Conrad in a sleepy voice, "Are we called out?"

"No, no, Conrad. I had a dream."

"Where are you going?"

"For air. Go back to sleep."

He stepped into the dark and strapped on his sword.

"I question God. That is my sin. That I cannot surrender to Him, obey Him as I do von Schnabelberg, is my sin. That God's will is not my will is my sin. God's will is like deep fog to me, a fog where I wander alone." Rudolf felt a knot of loss rise from his chest and spill forward in tears. He fell on his knees.

"God help me," he spoke aloud, not even a prayer. His head was bowed until, sensing light, he looked up to see the moon rising over the sea. The thin and twisted desert shrubs in front of him seemed, in the pale moonlight, like hands, extending broken claws across the sky. The times when the darkness of his soul had eclipsed the day of life, he had seen this as if from the bottom of a twilit hole, the branches of winter trees reaching across the opening to close him in. He shook his head to dispel the image, as he had learned to do, but this time the image remained.

He looked hard at the black-fingered shadows cast against the sand. They moved. Mixed with shadows were the sinewy shadow-shapes of serpents that came out in the night to hunt. Rudolf stared. Their slim tongues probed the air, looking for heat, and finding him, moved forward. He remained still, paralyzed. Then, in an action not even of his own choosing, he slowly and gently drew his sword and thrust it hard into the sand in front of him. "No," he said softly. The serpents – startled and frightened by the gesture, bewildered by the cold metal between them and the hopeful heat they had detected – branched back, curled in on themselves and retreated.

Rudolf stood, dazed. Was that all that was needed? A simple refusal? A sword in the sand? He turned toward camp and was surprised to see activity. It was still dark; the momentary brightness of the moon on the horizon, reflected in the sea, was over. Stars were bright overhead. He hurried to find his brother was already armed and waiting for him.

"Where did you go?" Conrad demanded.

"What has happened?"

"It is beginning," said Conrad. "Finally." Spies had brought news that Baibars was planning to attack – no one knew when, only that it would be soon. Desperate, hysterical, grief-driven, the leaders of the military orders abandoned the strategy of waiting and decided to strike first, leaving a comparatively defensible position for one that was not. They hoped the surprise of the attack would make up for the disadvantages of the location, but how could the enemy be surprised by anything on that all too open plain? "Hurry, Rudolf. Your horse is being saddled. Mine is ready."

Rudolf looked blankly at his brother's black horse with its head lowered to the ration of grain Conrad had given him.

"Go."

Rudolf went inside the tent. He had slept – and walked – in his shirt and hose. He found his felt tunic and slipped it over his head. His mail leggings were soon strapped on.

"Brother," called Conrad. "Do you need help? Your horse is ready." Indeed, Sir Adelbert's gray stallion stood waiting for his rider.

Rudolf came out holding the heavy mail. Conrad took it from him and held it so Rudolf could get inside. "Do you have your gloves?"

A horn sounded. It was the call they had waited for.

Conrad got on his black horse and reached forward to pat the horse's shoulder. Watching, Rudolf thought of the love his brother bore the animal beneath him. The green damp woods and his father's small castle were so far away; the infancy of the stallion was part of the dim past with their own childhood, memories like dreams.

The dead hot wait had ended. They had not come so far for these inert and suffocating days, camped within sight of the enemy. They had come for the promise of flags above the sea, for a life that would end in something more than "Alas!" They had come for the glory of God. "Ha! Rudolf! Finally!" he shouted, a wild an eager grin across his face. He set his helmet on his head, readying the faceplate, and drew on his mail gauntlets. "Rudolf! What say you now?"

Rudolf's feelings were not like Conrad's. The hallucinatory experience in the desert held him fast. Was that all that was needed? A simple no? How could it be so easy?

***

All of this journey had been an adventure for Conrad; he had reveled in the new sights, been quickened, awakened by the sounds of languages he could not understand, of foods he had never tried, of brightly colored spices that frightened Rudolf in the intoxication of their fragrance. For Conrad nothing was dangerous; nothing was evil; he was innocent in his curiosity.

He had found a bronze-skinned whore in Venice, with the nipples of her breasts large brown aureoles pushed against the soiled yellow silk of her gown; he had stared at this in fascination. As he stared, she had come up to him as cleanly and openly as the sun rising and taken his hand. Rudolf had followed his brother up the narrow lane to the small apartment where the girl both lived and worked. He stood outside waiting as the late afternoon slid into dusk. When Conrad did not appear, Rudolf, worried that there were others inside who would hurt his brother or steal from him, went to the opening and lifted the leather curtain that served as a door. He was stunned to see the two of them sitting on her low bed eating a meal of bread, fruit, wine and cheese. They were laughing, in lively conversation, though they had no common language. She spoke her Venetian dialect to Conrad who responded in Latin mixed with German slang. "Come in, brother," he said, looking up. Using his sleeve, Conrad wiped from his chin the juice of a plum he had just eaten. "Have one." He held a plum out to his brother.

Rudolf's heart was pounding. "Conrad," he said, hoarse, almost unable to speak, "have you?"

"No, brother. You know we have taken vows."

"But?"

"Isn't she lovely? Look at her! Look at those beautiful breasts," he said to Rudolf in German.

Rudolf was weighted down by the guilt he felt for having allowed his brother to enter the hut without him. Seeing that he was determined to go in, Rudolf knew he should have gone in, too. He knew the *Rule of Fraternal Correction* that sent all of them out into the streets of strange cities in pairs, or groups of three or four:

If you should detect this wantonness of the eye ... in any member of your brotherhood, forthwith admonish him that the evil thus begun may not grow worse but may be corrected by your charity...you cannot be free from blame if by your silence you allow your brethren to perish, when by pointing out their faults you might have corrected them. For if your brother had some bodily wound which he wished to hide through fear of the surgeon's knife, would it not be cruel to keep silence and merciful to reveal the wound?

He had not tried hard enough. He would try now. "That is sin, too, Conrad, your lust. It is as if you…"

"In truth, brother?"

"Yes. It is all the same to God. If you take her or simply want to take her, you have broken your vow to Christ. You know this, Conrad. Come with me now; leave this place. It is full of danger."

Conrad looked down for a moment, puzzling something through in his mind. "Rudolf, think you we will die on this journey, as father warned?"

"I cannot say, Conrad. Many men have."

"And if we die on this venture, we die in a state of grace. Is that not so?" Conrad crossed himself.

"Yes, of course."

"Well, then, brother, since I have sinned in looking at her as I have…" Conrad looked at the little whore again. She was small and brown and plump, as ripe and promising as the plum he had offered his brother. He paused and smiled.

"Conrad, come. For you to go forward will hurt us both, and do no good to her." Rudolf reached for his brother's sleeve. Conrad grinned and jumped up, evading Rudolf's hand.

Conrad handed his brother a sweet fig from the bowl. "Here, brother, taste this and then consider; would not life lose something had you never tried that fruit?"

Rudolf left the hut, feeling much as Conrad had at the fair when watching his black colt canter off with von Schnabelberg on his back. Unthinking, he clenched his fist around the fig. Surprised by the sensation, he opened his hand and stared blankly at the smashed fruit. Its ten thousand tiny seeds, carried by sweet, sticky pink juice, dripped through his fingers.

***

Rudolf rode to the front of his unit as it formed ranks behind him, making the most of the fragile dim safety of the hour before dawn. He looked at them as they were assembled, white mantles, one after the other, the black cross on their left shoulder; a cross embroidered on their white tunics and painted on their shields, broadswords buckled at their waists. Once his men were in ranks, he turned and got in place beside his brother. Flag bearers carried the white flag with the blood-red cross; others bore the double eagle of the Emperor or the colors of their families. They were assembled beneath a vast line of crosses held high, running the length of the mounted army.

"We do not choose this," said the Grand Marshal. "The infidel has forced us by breaking the peace. We go into battle in defense of the Holy Faith and the Holy City. Before us ride the Knights of St. Lazarus; then we, the Hospitallers and the Poor Knights will ride together. The forces of the enemy are greater, but their cause is Satan's, and in a fight with God, Satan cannot win. Why do we fight?"

The crowd called out as one:

We fight for the honor of the most glorious Virgin,
The mother of our Lord Jesus Christ,
For the honor and defense of the Holy Church
And for all the Christian faith
And for the expulsion of the enemies of the Cross!

Gott mit uns!

The priest prayed for God's blessing and led them all in the *Pater Noster*. The minnesinger who had come with them – himself a knight – broke open the morning with his clear voice. Others picked up the thread and sang:

Now my life has gained some meaning
Since these sinful eyes behold
The sacred land with meadows greening

Whose renown is often told.
This was granted me from God:
To see the land, the holy sod,
Which in human form He trod...
Christians, Jews, Muslims contending,
Claim it as a legacy
May God judge with grace unending
Through His blessed Trinity.
Strife is heard on every hand:
Ours the only just demand,
He will have us rule the land.

Conrad reached for Rudolf's gloved hand as it rested on the pommel of his saddle. Rudolf looked at his brother, seeing through the slits in his helmet mask the bright gleam in Conrad's blue eyes. Here at last was the great adventure for which Conrad had yearned. They rode inland, and when the moment came, it broke like fever. Conrad and Rudolf fought side-by-side lifting and dropping the blades of their swords against the surging enemy. Sound of metal against metal gave way to screaming, the heavy thud of falling men and horses, and the brothers moved on, and then, in the whirling dust, Rudolf could see Conrad no more.

Chapter 12, Jerusalem

Before the day was over, Rudolf stood alone as large birds swung wide arcs above the feast. All he knew was that he was not to be eaten. Jackals approached, heads and noses low, inching toward the corpses. Wounded horses thrashed. Dying horses screamed. The blood of infidel flowed into the blood of Christian converging in narrow streams, winding toward incarnadine pools where heavy flesh and armor pressed into the sand. Rudolf saw no living men. He had fallen into Hell and his punishment was the desperate isolation of his own survival.

The battle had begun with a terrifying and prophetic beauty; the enemy charged, hundreds of Khwaresmians on horseback, their lances strung with long, blood-red streamers, met first by the sad vanguard of the Leper Knights of St. Lazarus, the undimmed courage of the living dead. Behind came the rest, the Hospitallers, Templars and Teutonic Knights – nearly six thousand -- leveling their lances and raising their swords to meet the oncoming horsemen, shouting together, "*Gott min uns!*" The entire engagement was swift and deadly, and the streams beneath Rudolf's feet too soon replaced the infidel's scarlet ribbons. Where were those impassioned horsemen now? Where was his brother?

From horizon to horizon was death, body on body lying as they had fallen.

Rudolf turned and walked away though he had no place to go. If he were killed, all the better. At first, he trod carefully, as if some little bit of a man remained within the headless stabbed and bleeding bodies, the scattered limbs, but the dead numbered in the thousands, gruesome pavement over uneven ground, and so finally he walked where and how he could. A distance quickly spanned on horseback was now interminable. This morning's haunting vision and its message had been sent a long time ago; this walk was never to end.

Behind him, fire glowed against the smoke mixed with fog coming from the sea. The camp in which he had awakened that morning was burning; bodies were burning. Shapes and voices came and went in the darkness and mist. He reached the Jerusalem road without knowing where he was, only thinking that he must move. His mind tried to work out something of the actual passing of time. When exactly was it that he and the others had ridden down from Acre? How long had they camped? How long had they waited?

He felt his injury, a sword slash to his leg, which, in the night, reached a high arc of pain. After that, his leg stiffened around his suffering. He abandoned his shirt of mail. His helmet had fallen somewhere. He wore only the breeches, the felt vest and long shirt that went beneath. His flesh and his clothing were covered in dust and blood. His black hair was roped and tangled like that of any haggard war-weary refugee. Nothing remained to distinguish him as a member of one side or the other. There were hundreds of such wanderers. Some were cut down by shrilly screaming passing riders, but most were ignored. Where had they all come from?

Rudolf walked all night. When the sun rose high, and the desert heat filled the world, he rolled into the ditch beside the road and lay inert, hypnotized by exhaustion but not sleeping. The dead lay all around and his camouflage was that he appeared to be yet one more body. He noticed nothing -- not the rotting smell, not the flies, not the passing soldiers. When night came, his wounded leg protested fiercely when he tried to stand, and he screamed in spite of his parched throat. For so long there had been so much screaming that one more scream excited no notice. Pushed by something beyond his will, he, who had so often wished to die, stood firm against death without knowing why. The will of the flesh moved him, and he continued on. The third night of his wandering, dehydrated and exhausted, Rudolf reached Jerusalem and walked through David's gate, unthinking, one of a crowd of returning Muslim refugees with their carts and goats and families.

This was no golden city. It was the same dust, the same clay, the same crowds, the same fetid odors as every other place. Fear and the hysteria of fatigue overcame him as he tried to run through the tangle of streets. Coming in was easy enough, but now, how to get out? When he stopped to catch his breath, he saw not far ahead of him an open gate in the disordered heap of rubble that had been Jerusalem's wall. If no one stopped him, he would be free of this city at least, though what lay beyond he could not know.

Seeing Baibar's men guarding the opening, Rudolf hesitated. His back against a wall, he looked sideways toward the gate.

"Why am I running?" he thought suddenly. "I did not come here to live. I came here to die." This sinful thought frightened him, and he began to cross himself, but then remembered where he was, unwittingly choosing an action of survival. Waves of sorrow flowed through his mind, his heart, his flesh. He – who had come yearning not for salvation but for death – was alive. Conrad – who had come with the full force of his passion for life -- was most likely dead. In a spasm of pain, Rudolf hunched over, and his empty belly discharged green bile. The sound of his retching drew the attention of a guard, who watched for a moment then said something to his companion. Rudolf wiped his mouth with the back of his hand, straightened his back and walked as if there were no guards, no future, no dread. The guards who had watched his futile vomiting looked into his face and shrugged. Such a thing as he, limping, retching, unarmed and exhausted, was nothing to worry about.

The open gate led to a courtyard. To one side was a cistern. He dropped his goatskin bag into the water, withdrew it and drank. The sudden relief shocked his body and he retched again, the cool water coming back up. He drank again, this time more slowly, and felt the water slide down his throat and knew that this time it would stay.

Looking around, Rudolf saw that the place was a hospital. The hospital and its attendant convent made a permanent island of truce during all fighting, a truce honored even by the rapacious Khwaresmians. The building, the steps and small courtyard in front – in which a fire burned – were packed with groaning men, women and children who had been caught in the fighting somewhere. Could

Conrad be here? How would he have made his way? He could not. Rudolf knew then, for sure. He could not have been carried; had he been hurt and on foot, Rudolf would have seen him. If, by miraculous chance, Conrad were there, he would die or he would recover. They would find each other. There were few ports from which they could sail. Ships came in and out of Acre taking Europeans away, bringing Europeans in, carrying items for trade in both directions. It was a funnel through which the two worlds flowed.

A man in the robes of a prior spoke to him. "Do you need help, brother?" His voice was hoarse, scratchy, as if his throat were on fire. When he inhaled, a whistle came from his chest.

"Are you speaking to me?" asked Rudolf in German. He did not think. No one had spoken to him in three days.

The priest repeated his question, this time in German. At the sound of his own language, Rudolf felt overwhelmingly sad. "No, Father. I am…" Rudolf could not finish. The priest had reached a hand toward him; the hand was but a stump, his gesture a thoughtless reflex at hearing the sounds of home.

Rudolf looked at him bewildered, then frightened. He turned away and continued along what had once been the city wall, but before he had gone far, he collapsed, unconscious from hunger, exhaustion and pain, only a few yards from the courtyard of the Lazarite hospital.

He awoke in the hospital courtyard on a pallet of clean and folded rags beside others like him, all shaded by a linen canopy. Hearing him groan, a nun came to him and asked him in French if he could eat. Rudolf nodded. In hungry draughts, he drank the soup she gave. His wound was cleaned and wrapped with linen bandages. Still, after two days, and in spite of the protesting nuns, Rudolf decided to leave. The pain had subsided, and he believed he could walk. His goatskin bag filled with water, and carrying piles of bread from the hospital ovens, he left, following the road north.

Chapter 13, Escape

The peace of the body then consists in the duly proportioned arrangement of its parts...and that of the rational soul the harmony of knowledge and action. The peace of body and soul is the well-ordered and harmonious life and health of the living creature. Peace between man and God is the well-ordered obedience of faith to eternal law. St. Augustine, *City of God*

Rudolf's fear that he would be seen and seized vanished on the road north to Nablus. The inland route to Acre was filled with refugees, a population of pain struggling to move.

The French-speaking nurse had given Rudolf a crutch when he left the hospital, along with the warning that it would be better for him to stay until his wound had drained completely and scar tissue covered it.

"Stay where you are safe. Since the days of Saladin, our hospital has been a place for all to come without fear. But," said the nurse, "your mind is still in the battle. You don't know that no one is pursuing or attacking you. There is no fight. It is over, young lord. Quiet your mind and let your leg heal."

She was right. Rudolf's mind ran along the track of the battle unable to sort through the terrifying overload of impressions, the sounds, the screaming horses and the shrill wail of their Bedouin allies as they fled at the sight of the Khwaresmians. It had happened in an instant. "Stand your ground, men!" called out von Schnabelberg to the rest of them. "*Gott min uns!*"

What if they had waited, held fast on the sand until the Khwaresmians gave up in disgust at the futility, but de Brienne, his mind half-derailed, had not waited.

"*Gott min Uns!*"

God where?

God was with them, all of them, lying on the sand. "God is with them," thought Rudolf, "and I remain."

His eyes filled with tears.

"If you can wait, young lord," continued the nurse, "you will be as good as new. Your injury is not serious, and the only danger is infection. Your leg needs attention and care. Rest, young lord." Her world was death, but this one was not doomed to die; this one she could help.

Each day a cart went around the wall to Jerusalem's charnel house outside the city gates. For weeks past, the cart had been filled to overflowing. She shook her head against this image.

"Where do you come from, young lord?" she asked.

"Castle Lunkhofen, near Affoltern, a village over the Albis Mountains, not far from Zürich."

The woman nodded.

"Do you know it?" asked Rudolf, confused by her gesture.

"No, no. I come from Troyes. I have never been – until I came here – away from home. " As a young girl she had dreamt that Christ had reached for her hand and drawn her behind him to a place of great and hopeless suffering. All around were knights carrying the cross. When she awoke, she knew she must go to Jerusalem and there she must remain. She took the cross herself and joined a pilgrim's caravan to Acre. On the galley was a monk who, in imitation of St. Martin, sought to help those who were farthest from God, those shoved to the boundaries by mankind in its fear, the lepers. "Come with me," he had said. "There is a hospital in Jerusalem where you can help those who need help most."

The work of helping the hopeless lifted and inspired her, but as treaties were broken and alliances changed, the population of the hospital was now mostly the wounded and those dying of wounds.

"You could die if the wound becomes septic," she said as she wiped Rudolf's brow with a cool cloth.

He could not disagree. He had seen enough himself, but still he would go. His own death was nothing. He understood it would happen, and afterward he would see nothing.

***

Many of the wells along the route had been poisoned – easy enough to distinguish them now from the absence of refugees camping around them. The sorry caravan trudged on, glassy-eyed and exhausted. Most had no idea where they were going. There was nothing behind them; of what lay in front of them, they had no knowledge. Some pulled carts that held their possessions. Some carried bundles. Most were empty-handed.

"Khwaresmians," they said, passing a burned out village, its road lined with heads elevated on poles, its well filled with bodies. It didn't matter what these people named their god or the shape of the ritual by which He was worshipped. Everyone fell together on a dusty road and those who survived walked together as brothers.

Rudolf leaned on his crutch and walked with as much speed and vigor as he could. His goal was Starkenberg, the castle fortress belonging to the Teutonic Knights. And from there? He hoped to return to battle.

A man from Basel had joined the refugees soon after leaving Jerusalem. He was older than Rudolf and had survived the capture of Jerusalem, though he had lost everything, his wife, children, business and his right hand. "Why do you not leave?" the man asked Rudolf. "You can get a berth on a galley and go home. For my part, I am going to Jaffa. I can get passage from there. I want away from this place. There is nothing here now."

He held the stump up in the air as he walked and explained to Rudolf how, when he held it down at his side, his vanished hand felt as if it were burning. The moment the infidel had sliced through his arm, he had thrust the bleeding stump into the fire to prevent infection. "We cannot beat them. This is their world, not ours. There are many of them; there will never be many of us."

"Why did you come here?"

"I owned a hostel for pilgrims not far from the Church of the Holy Sepulcher. It served my family very well, but…" he shook his head. "What of you?"

"My younger brother and I took the cross. Two years ago? More? We joined others in Acre and then the rest of them near Gaza. I led a company. We attacked the infidel. When they rode at us, most of our army – Bedouins – ran. We were outnumbered, facing the enemy. Thousands of them all mounted, and we? Not a tenth of their forces. When it was over, I saw no other survivors." Rudolf could speak of it in a flat calm voice, but inside? A question without answer sickened him. "I left the battlefield alone. In three days time, I was in Jerusalem, in a leper hospital, yet all around me were wounded men and women and children. I stayed two days there."

"What of your brother?"

Rudolf looked at the man. "I do not know what happened to him or where he is."

"Did you search for him?"

Rudolf slowly shook his head. The gravity of his admission filled his heart with lead. "Everywhere were bodies, legs, heads, each sinking into the sand. Piles of bodies, each like the next, nameless arms and legs and heads, whole men face down, their skulls crashed in or cut in two, one atop the other. Night was falling, and I was alone."

"Jerusalem was so when I fled," said the man, "but at last I found my wife, my little girl. You might have more peace now if you knew where your brother was, where he had fallen, if he fell."

Rudolf was already half consumed in smoldering guilt; the man's questions blew the coals to life. The open desert was not the same place as a walled city when it came to looking for one's dead, but Rudolf said nothing. He did not speak of his numbness or the fear that broke it open. He could still see the circling arcs of vultures, the bent necks and drooping heads of wild dogs as they moved closer in the gathering dusk, the day spent in a ditch along the Jerusalem road beside the dead, hearing through his dim sleep the howl of jackals.

"The next morning? Could you not have looked then?"

Rudolf closed his eyes for a moment. Who was this man? Conscience or companion? He shook his head. "I only thought to move." Rudolf felt a pang of shame. Perhaps he would have found Conrad in the silence of morning.

The Baseler, seeing how his questions had hurt the boy, let the subject go. "Will you return home now?" he asked.

"No," answered Rudolf, softly, resigned. "You?"

"I will. God willing, my parents are still alive, and I can yet care for them in their old age. I will try again to build a life, and this time in my own country. One hand or two, it will be the same. I will put myself into it by finding a small inn or tavern to run on a pilgrim road. I can offer advice and shelter to those on their way here, and consolation and shelter to those who are returning."

Hunger and sorrow had inscribed lines on the man's face, characteristic of sad old men. Yet his back was straight and his voice young.

"There is nothing for me at home now," Rudolf replied. "I have made a vow, and it is best for me to stay until I have fulfilled it." Both men wanted to expiate the guilt of survival, though Rudolf did not hope to find a way. No less than Cain, he was his brother's killer. He no longer recalled Conrad's determination and enthusiasm. Rudolf had forgotten how Conrad had longed for battle, their arguments about jousting, everything. He remembered only that morning Conrad had taken care of his horse before his own, that Conrad had put his brother first out of love and respect for his higher rank. He remembered how he had left Conrad to sin in Venice. In Rudolf's confused mind, Conrad had followed him out into the world just as when he was a small child, he had followed Rudolf everywhere he went, mimicking his walk, speech and every small gesture.

"Watch your brother," his mother bade him over and over during the years that Heinrich was gone. "He is wild and could hurt himself. Take care of him." Rudolf had grabbed his chubby, fair-haired brother by the hand and taken him outside and showed him how to make a toy bow with a green branch and some string. He and

Conrad ran through the forest surrounding the castle with these toys, hunting the wild boars of the imagination. Rudolf was faster and did not notice that his brother was no longer behind him. He hid behind a wide tree in ambush, pretending to be a wild pig, but Conrad did not come. Rudolf ran back calling for Conrad and almost reached the castle without finding him. Rudolf hurried back into the forest, calling, but his voice was lost in the dampening foliage and muffled by his tears. At dusk, a terrified Rudolf returned to the castle to his enraged mother.

"He said you ran away from him. How could you do that? What kind of monster are you?" Part of Anna's reaction was simply relief at seeing her older son home safely. "Go away. I cannot stand the sight of you right now. Go. Pray God to give you a real heart."

Again he had abandoned his brother in the forest. Rudolf's mind had begun spinning a net of illusion that would convince him that it was his own dark confusion that had led Conrad to that battlefield. Rudolf looked at the dusty road. He had wanted to die, and then he had lived. He had fought for his life even against his will. Others died; his brother died, in his stead.

Looking into Rudolf's eyes, the man saw something terrible and dark that made him reluctant to leave Rudolf on this road. "Men die in battle. You could have died yourself. It was not as if the risk was not the same for all. You did not die; that is all. You bear no responsibility for those who died. There is nothing more God or anyone could expect of you. Come back with me. If we stay together, it will go easier for us. You must do what you must," said the man gently. "But if you come with me you will be in Jaffa soon, and there someone can care for your leg."

"I cannot climb that hill," Rudolf said, looking at the ridge across which he could already see the Jaffa road.

"I will help you. You can lean on me."

"You are not strong," said Rudolf. The man's kindness deepened Rudolf's contempt for himself. The leg now throbbed in a strange rhythm of pain, excruciating when he placed his weight on it. He looked down from time to time at the dressing through which red blood had begun to seep. This was what the nurse had feared, that the wound would open.

***

Night brought them to an empty village. They built small fires and settled in the square around the well, taking turns at watch. A few hours before dawn, Rudolf was awakened. Struggling to his feet, his leg on fire, he cried out loudly in surprise and pain. "You are badly hurt," said the woman who had awakened him.

"No, it's nothing, nothing. I had forgotten; that's all. Help me to stand."

She held out her forearm, hand clenched in a fist, and Rudolf reached for it. As he rose, she backed away slowly. "Thank you," he said, reaching for his crutch. Sweat covered his face.

"You need not," she said. "There are others. I am not tired, and I can watch longer. Do not if it pains you so."

"It is nothing. Get some sleep."

From the bench that stood beside the well, he looked at the horizon above the smoke and dust. Off into the night, he saw still more fires to scare off the jackals and other beasts. Sad groups looking for safety littered the whole upside-down world. Rudolf knew little about the politics that had led to this, how the Christian Army had surrendered the Holy City on the gamble of ultimately gaining both Egypt and Jerusalem. All was still; the horizon sat unmoving.

He looked straight above him into the moonless night, the stars brighter than they ever shone at home. "It is the same sky," he thought, picking out constellations. "Am I the same man?"

It was late on one of winter's short afternoons some years past when he and Conrad had ridden away from von Schnabelberg's castle. "You are starting out late, boys," the duke had warned. "Stay the night." Conrad was fierce; there was a tournament in the wide plain near Dübelstein, and he had put himself in to ride. It would be the first time the black horse – or Conrad -- would ride against another.

"We will make it at least partway. Then, by first light, we can be off again and reach Dübelstein in time."

"Conrad, our father would not like it, and this is a lie. He will have us with von Schnabelberg until tomorrow."

"Exactly. He need never know."

"He would forbid you, Conrad. You know that. Knowing that, you should not ride, and we should stay here."

"He won't know, Rudolf. Don't worry about it."

"You think he won't find out? Certainly he will find out."

"By then I will have ridden."

"You could be killed, Conrad. Would you risk that?"

"Killed? I won't be killed."

"And if I stay here?"

"Then I go alone." Conrad had grinned widely at his older brother. He was reasonably certain Rudolf would not let him ride off alone. "Why don't you ride, too?"

"No. It's foolish; such things are foolish. That's why they have been forbidden."

"And yet you are a knight."

"Courage, Conrad," he said, "is not proven by killing others."

"How often does anyone die?"

"Once is enough. And death is not the only outcome. You could be blinded, lose an arm or leg, or be left an idiot."

"You think I don't know that?"

Seeing no way to stop Conrad, Rudolf rode off with him through the winter night to the new-built walls of Dübelstein Castle, where, along with others who had put in for the tournament, they pitched a camp and slept until daylight. Ravaged by responsibility and guilt, Rudolf did not sleep, but Conrad slept the sleep of angels and awoke excited and happy at the thought of his first tournament.

The lists were called. Conrad and the black horse ran. Conrad unhorsed his man in one brilliant rapid ride. When Conrad took off his helmet, Rudolf saw pure joy on his brother's face. He wasn't thinking that his opponent – a childhood friend – could have been killed by the force of the lance. They rode home, Rudolf knowing all of this, his father knowing nothing; another sin into which he had allowed his brother to fall.

Word of Conrad's success, and of Lunkhofen's horse, reached Heinrich before the boys did. Heinrich was furious, mostly because of the risk to the horse. "You, Conrad, you know what that horse represents. How could you take such a risk? Thank the good Lord for your luck this time. He knows you have little enough skill or experience!" He said nothing to Rudolf, simply looked at him and shrugged. Deep down, he was glad to have the horse tested, and he in no way blamed his older son. He knew how headstrong Conrad was.

Anna saw it differently and railed at Rudolf for allowing his brother to ride.

"If you had stayed behind, Conrad would have stayed, too. I doubt he would have ridden alone through the night."

"Mother," said Rudolf, "*you* try to stop him when he has his heart set. Von Schnabelberg could not hold him back, and when I tried, Conrad laughed at me. I could not let him go alone."

"He would not have ridden, Rudolf."

"Mother, he had already signed up for the lists!"

"Be that as it may, had you stayed with von Schnabelberg, Conrad would have stayed."

"Mother, Conrad was going with or without me."

"I wonder that you argue with me. You don't think I know my own son? Conrad is obedient and loving. He does not argue with me."

"No. He tells you what you want to hear, and then does what he wants."

"He is not half the liar you are, Rudolf. I know the true face behind all your devotion and solicitude." At that, she turned, and swept from the room. Rudolf was left, his sense of what was real quavering and dim.

She had been so angry and nothing had happened to Conrad. And now? Conrad had ridden again at an enemy, and the outcome was different.

***

Dawn began, a bright line of blue in the east bringing Rudolf back from his memories. He called out to the others, "Morning." Someone's caged rooster crowed as evidence. The travelers stretched, coughed and stood, shook some of the dust from their bedding and put their things in order. Rudolf dropped the big goatskin bag into the well, pulled it up and from it filled his own. He dropped the bag down again and filled the bag of another man who had come, and so he continued until all had water for at least the first part of the day. There was no food. Some washed the tired dust from their faces; most didn't bother. There would be more, and then more yet, as the days ahead unwound their journey.

That night they reached Nablus, attacked by the Khwaresmians months before, and camped. Rudolf's leg no longer hurt. The blood on the dressing dried, and he left it. Perhaps it was healing on its own. He did not know that the wound had filled with pus, and what drained into the dressing now was simply too thick to penetrate the layers of blood-crusted linen gauze. The wound sat in its own putrescence.

"You can join your Order at Acre, young lord. That's but three more days. You need not go all the way to Starkenberg," said an old man who had not before spoken to Rudolf. The man, who traveled with two children, and Rudolf now made up the back of the caravan. The six-year-old girl had gone part of the way on the old man's shoulders. The boy was old enough to understand what had happened to his life, his parents, his world. Wearing sorrow's thin-lipped stoicism, he walked in determination and silence beside his guardian. The children would return with the man to his village near Munich.

"You can go to them. They will help you, care for you."

Rudolf shook his head. "There is no one there, a few monks, some disabled knights, perhaps, if they have not gone home. There is a prior left behind by God; that is all there was when we rode from there yesterday."

"Yesterday? Yesterday we were at Nazareth."

"Indeed no," said Rudolf. "We rode behind von Schnabelberg and stopped at Caesarea."

"Young lord, stop a moment."

Rudolf stopped and stood still. The old man reached for Rudolf's forehead. Even before he touched it, he felt the heat radiating from it. "You are very ill. You must stop with us at Acre. You must get help."

"There is no help," said Rudolf. "Everyone is dead."

"I am sure you are wrong. At the very least the prior and the priests will be there, those who are needed to care for the ill and injured, the hospital, those men will be there."

"None of them is alive. I watched them fall on the battlefield. All save I." Rudolf's voice was strained and bewildered; tears ran down his cheeks carving rivers of pink in the crust of dirt.

"At the very least, the Hospitallers will have room for us, or," and he crossed himself, "the Lazarites, though God willing we need not go there. Someone will certainly help us. You cannot imagine you are the only survivor?"

"Can you not see it yourself? The vultures are everywhere pecking out their eyes."

***

Exhausted, with safety in sight, food and care and the chance to return to their home countries, the travelers no longer thought about the disaster in the city of Jerusalem or all their losses. The five days' journey and its perils had all but cleaned their minds and hearts of past suffering. They would remember later, but for the moment the forward momentum of escape held them above despair.

The old man set down the little girl and reached for Rudolf's arm. "Come home with me, young lord. It is not so far from Bavaria to the Rhine. And here in Acre, we will wait until we find good passage. Come with us. Think of your mother and father and how they will rejoice to have you with them again."

"My brother is dead."

"We all die, young lord. That is the least surprising thing in our lives. Your parents will understand the risks of battle."

"I have killed him."

"How is that? Did he not take the same vow as you, to offer his life for the Holy Cross? It is not your will, but God's will that decides these things."

"No, no, my brother wanted to stay home with his horse, but I had to come. You are looking at Satan," he said, pointing at his breast. "I came to die, but my brother died."

"Take his hand," the old man said to the little girl. "Maybe he will let you lead him." And to Rudolf he said, "Take her hand, young lord. I cannot carry her any longer. Help her walk into the city so she can find again her family and her home."

Rudolf looked down at the fair-haired little girl beside him. She looked up at him, her sweet brown eyes with their dark lashes offering him all the trust in the universe.

When he looked at her, he thought he saw Gretchen; he imagined her saying, *Do you really love me so much, Rudolf?*

"I never knew happiness like this existed, Gretchen. Your hand in mine? Our future? All is possible in this world. I can believe that with you here beside me."

"My dear love," she sighed and laid her head against his shoulder.

The old man hoped that in helping another, Rudolf's darkness would dissolve; he did not know all the traps in Rudolf's memory. When Rudolf fell, it was with the little girl's hand against his heart.

The group stopped.

"He is very ill," said a woman who had come with them all the way from Jerusalem.

"He is at the end of his reason," said the old man.

"So I feared," said the woman. "Let me look at his wound. Here, move aside a bit. Have you water to spare?"

"And then what will you do? Have you a way to redress it? Leave it," said a young priest. "We are within sight of the city. Leave him here and come back with help, a litter and perhaps a doctor."

"There is reason in that. Do you think he will regain consciousness now?"

"His body has provided for him this oblivion, to recover or to die." The old man looked down at Rudolf's prone form.

"I will stay with him," said the priest.

They left Rudolf and the priest behind and entered Acre, unprepared for what they found. There was no help for Rudolf, no young men to carry a litter out to the desert to rescue yet one more fallen soldier; there was nothing. The Orders were badly weakened. Their leaders were dead or captured and their manpower reduced almost to nothing. Though the busy port city was doing business more or less as usual, the castles of the military orders were nearly empty.

As dark approached, the priest was forced to decide to act on his own behalf or on behalf of the unconscious, fallen young man. The priest's journey had had its own Hells. The ugly specter of cowardice and failure tore at him. He had watched as Khwaresmians stripped and raped all the women and girls who had run into the church for safety. He had seen the sacramental objects desecrated by laughing wild tribesmen urinating on the holy altar. Through all, he had hidden himself for his own safety, and had survived. His terror was that he felt no remorse, no guilt, for saving his own life as others died, that he had taken no action to protect the objects of his faith from the infidel's foul hands. However he may have been horrified at his own selfishness, he had plumbed the depths of his nature.

"Good luck, my friend. Would that I had more to offer you right now, but perhaps you are sliding into God's own world, and my help would hinder your journey and the peace awaiting you there." He made the sign of the cross over Rudolf's unconscious form and turned toward Acre.

***

Rudolf came back to consciousness in the heat of the sun. He had lain unmolested through the night, one more fallen refugee left for dead. He pulled himself to his feet and started walking.

The road to Starkenberg was wide and well traveled, but where Rudolf should have turned and headed for the coast, he did not. He too often forgot to drink. His companions were hallucinations and memories; he lived with no sense of time. At times he rode beside Conrad. Other times, he rode alone. Sometimes, in his stumbling delirium, he held Gretchen's hand. Sometimes he watched the dim image of his mother walk into an endless hallway and though he followed, calling out to her, she never turned.

After two days, he found a small stream in a narrow valley, and, taking it for a familiar stream in the forest surrounding Castle Lunkhofen, he dropped to his belly and thrust in his head. It cooled his steaming face and for the moment brought him to himself, but when he tried to use his leg to get up off the ground, he fainted under the pain.

Book Three: Truth

Chapter 14, Youhanna

The light of your grace plainly shone in him… By now he was an old man and I thought that in all the long years he had spent to such good purpose in following your way he must have gained great experience and much knowledge, as indeed he had. I hoped that if I put my problems to him, he would draw upon his experience and his knowledge to show me how best a man in my state of mind might walk upon your way. St. Augustine, *Confessions*

"Bless the Lord, O my soul, O Lord my God…who coverest thyself with light as with a garment: who stretchest out the heavens like a curtain; who layeth the beams of his chambers in the waters: who maketh clouds his chariot: who walketh upon the wings of the wind." Youhanna saluted the Lord this morning as he did all others. God had given him another day in which something might be done. Though still more dark than dawn, there was light enough for Youhanna to see something lying in the stream that did not belong.

Mulberry and olive trees ringed two small fields of grain. On one well-drained south-facing hillside was a vineyard, and between the hill and the fields ran the narrow wash. Youhanna focused on what seemed to be a man. Looking up and down the valley, Youhanna saw no army and no pilgrims. The man must be alone. Youhanna hurried along the ledge and down the switchbacks to the valley floor. Morning's sweet pure blue spread upwards, the sun a crimson promise on the edge of the world.

***

For weeks, Rudolf lay like an animal in the shelter of Youhanna's cave. His occupation, even against his will, was survival. His body fought to regain strength; his mind struggled within it, taking what it needed from silence and sleep. The edges of certainty on which he had walked all his life – believing they were the world's broad roads – had become with each turn more treacherous, more deceptive, narrower.

Rudolf could not know that more ships and young men were on their way. The Grand Master of the Hospitallers, who had survived the massacre in Jerusalem, had described the events vividly to the Pope. Though five-thousand had died that day on the battlefield at La Forbie, several hundred had been taken prisoner. Baibars demanded ransom. But for all Rudolf knew, everyone had died. Many others believed the same.

The Pope had then assembled a council and called for another crusade to avenge the deaths of his armies and the sack of Jerusalem.

***

Rudolf's exhausted mind dragged him into endless repetitions of the battle. The red ribbons tied to lances transformed instantly to flying plumes of blood. The wails of horses, screams of men, heads and limbs flying from bodies still holding to the seats on which they rode, headless horsemen careening to a halt and falling in slow motion, landing with heavy thumps in the all-receiving dust. Behind all, Rudolf heard the words of the minnesinger luring him, not to glory and salvation, but to death in this most strange of history's empty battles. "If I could make that beloved voyage across the sea, I would sing 'Joy!' and never more 'Alas'."

His father's words, "It is not glory, son. It is horror," mingled with his mother's, "And you left your little brother behind!" Rudolf struggled to wake, but in its need, his exhausted body clung to sleep.

Youhanna, who spent most of the night in prayer, heard Rudolf's involuntary, choking sobs, the lurching tremble of emotion breaking from his soul. Youhanna gently lifted Rudolf's head so that it rested on his knee. Rudolf stirred, murmuring, "I am sorry," in German.

***

When his wound closed and his fever came down, Rudolf walked along the ledge, first leaning on Youhanna and then alone with his crutch. In the pain and weakness of his leg, Rudolf felt his life as part of his body, something he had not felt before. Rudolf had lived mostly within the confines of his mind. "I am alive," he said with wonder. "But why?"

"Your soul is lonely. It is apart from God. That is all. You cry out in the night as many have before you; that you cry means you will find help." The hermit spoke some Latin, but not with the same ease as the educated European.

"I must simply wait, or, better, die. There is no help."

"Die?"

"Why am I not dead? I do not know how I came here, by what power or whose desire. It was not mine."

"God's."

"God's?"

"You doubt it?"

Rudolf fell back and curled into himself like an infant.

Youhanna took a deep breath and began to chant, "*I cried unto God with my voice, even unto God with my voice; and he gave ear unto me. In the day of my trouble I sought the Lord: my sore ran in the night and ceased not: my soul refused to be comforted. I remembered God and was troubled: I complained, and my spirit was overwhelmed. Thou holdest mine eyes waking: I am so troubled that I cannot speak...Will the Lord cast me off forever? And will he be favorable no more? Is his mercy clean gone forever? Doth his promise fail forevermore? Hath he in anger shut up his tender mercies? Then I said, this is my infirmity...I will remember the works of the Lord. I will meditate on thy work...Thou art the God that doest wonders'*. It is time you left this cave. Your leg is healed enough. Tomorrow, my boy, we will meditate on God's work."

***

Rudolf followed Youhanna down the mountain. He was weak, and his leg throbbed, though the wound had healed. It was a tight, angry-looking, red knot. He leaned on his crutch, and walked slowly down the several switchbacks. The sun rose, and Rudolf squinted against the harsh white light of morning. Halfway down, Youhanna turned onto a narrow trail that cut across the south face of the hillside. They were soon among grapevines, perhaps twenty rows of twelve, bare branches reaching from one to the other like dancers in a line. The rows were planted two arm's-lengths apart, providing an easy passageway for Youhanna and for air to circulate.

"It is in work we can fully understand the mystery of God's creation. What we struggle to accomplish, God need only think and it is there in perfection. He made us to tend His creation, to guide it lovingly, through our hands to imitate His hand. Our Lord himself has given us instruction, '*I am the true vine, and my Father is the husbandman. Every branch in me that beareth not fruit He taketh away; and every branch that beareth fruit He purgeth it that it may bring forth even more fruit...*' exactly as our Lord describes," said Youhanna. "We cut away the weak and the dead branches that next year the vines will yield more. We want the young grapes to be sheltered from the sun but not so much so that fungus grows on them. They must be stroked by the breezes, but not blown by the wind. Grapes are one of God's gifts to us, and they must be tended carefully." Rudolf watched as Youhanna worked rhythmically, confidently. When he had finished with a plant, its bare limbs drew a pattern of lace against the sky.

The work was difficult physically and demanded complete mental concentration, pulling Rudolf from his endless struggle with himself. All he need do was what Youhanna told him. At the end of that clear November afternoon, freed from himself, Rudolf looked up between the laced branches at a sky too blue, too pure to believe, and gasped. Youhanna looked over at him and saw what was written on his face. "Thank you, Lord," he said in silent prayer. "You have opened your eye to him."

***

"Faithful, infidel," Rudolf began, "one atop the other..." He stopped. "I knew only I had done this, that the men lying around me had fallen by my hand. I no longer knew why. All of them, all of them, are in Heaven and I..."

"How did you get so far from home?" Youhanna knew the answer, but he wanted Rudolf to talk.

"Priests came to the fair in my village. My father and brother were selling horses; I was with my mother." Rudolf's heart beat faster under the pressure of memory. "The priest – there were two, but one spoke – took the stage in the afternoon. They said our sins would be forgiven if we took the cross – we had heard it before. My father was seven years away from us in the crusade. For what? His sins? My mother would say his sin was leaving us."

Youhanna looked at Rudolf for a moment, gauging the depth of his struggle in the fullness of his voice. "Ah, and so you followed this priest and left your home behind?"

Rudolf nodded.

"But now you wonder. Was the priest right?"

Hearing this dangerous, secret question so clearly spoken, the lump that was Rudolf's heart opened. He nodded; his eyes filled with tears. What was next? What events? "The priests came to stay with us as our father's guests. There was a feast after the fair in the great hall of the castle and an argument between the mayor – who had been with my father in Damietta – and the duke, von Schnabelberg. Anyway, the mayor spoke out against the crusade, and the duke was insulted and left."

"What did he say?"

"Many things. Worst was that the duke did not know what he was talking about, that he had no experience. Von Schnabelberg was filled with courtesy. But inside me…" Rudolf broke off; he had no idea how to go on. There was nothing real he could say or point to. "Now the duke is dead." Rudolf closed his eyes and saw von Schnabelberg as they sat in the refectory in Acre, listening to the priest speak of the sack of Jerusalem. They had thought the priest worldly, cynical, but in the end, he had told the truth; his bitterness was only an aspect of what could not be changed. "I do not know if it was the taunting of the mayor that night, but the duke led us here. He saw something in Conrad, and he outfitted my brother, sponsored his knighthood. I was certain that coming here was the way for me.

In this crusade, as the priests had said, I would find peace for once and for all, to know… But what I know? It was not Heaven. It was all the mayor had said that night; it was Hell on earth."

"I have heard of a little priest who came from a foreign place and attempted to stand between the Egyptian and the Christian armies to stop the fighting," said Youhanna. "The Egyptian Sultan, Al Kamil, honored him, but the siege did not end. The Christians opened that city, finally, and bloated bodies of innocent children filled the streets."

"That would have been St. Francis. This my father described to me, but I would not listen. I, too, was angry with the mayor. I thought he did not understand that nothing of what he said mattered in comparison to fighting for Christ or for the fact that those who were there, dead or alive, were sure of Heaven. To risk my life for the sake of my soul? My life was nothing, even less than nothing in my eyes." Rudolf lay silent for a moment, gathering both his thoughts and his emotions. "The hope of Heaven? There was no Heaven there. Nothing Satan has for us could be worse."

Youhanna nodded. "But there is something worse than that. Hell is the absence of God."

"Then I have known it. God was nowhere to be found on that battlefield."

Youhanna looked sharply at Rudolf. "Despair is not the absence of God, my son. God is always there; we are simply blind."

Rudolf looked at the fire-shadows on the ceiling of the cave. If only he had that much light inside, just that, dim though it was. If he closed his eyes, he saw it all again; the minnesinger and his own parents' distracted looks, the triumph of the moment the knights had all met in Venice, the beautiful proud ship, the blood red cross painted on the sail. It seemed so long ago that he had thought of glorious death, redeemed, to live forever beside Christ or, if not that, to carry the day, then to return to Gretchen and home, his soul freed, his future peaceful. Had that been the reason? His own torn motive? He could not think of this clearly. "I did not fight for Christ. I fought to save myself. I lifted my sword and let fall my sword." He lifted his arm and in the air made the same hard cuts and thrusts he had taken into battle. "My sword worked of its own will – or the Devil's will – and now I am alive though all are dead. I do not even want this life." A sob caught his voice, and he dropped his arm and pounded his chest with his fist. "And yet it keeps beating, this empty thing."

"The psalmist has written, *'But I am a worm, and no man; a reproach of men and despised of the people.'* You are not the first to feel forsaken by God, to doubt yourself, your faith, your decisions. We live in darkness and yearn constantly for light. It is by God's will we are here, and this life we live is part of God's will."

"Is this God's will? My brother dead? He was so filled with life. And I?" He shook his head. Unconsciously, he waved a hand in front of his face as if to push the fog aside. 'We ride, Rudolf! Now we ride!' How could Conrad have felt joy and not dread in those moments? They all knew how outnumbered were their forces, and they wondered what Walter de Brienne was thinking, but he was the Master over all of them. Did Conrad even consider he might die?"

Tears escaped Rudolf's closed eyelids. Seeing them, Youhanna reached for Rudolf's hand, still a fist over his heart. At that, Rudolf's bitter resistance broke, and his tears flowed freely. He turned to his side and buried his face in the goatskin. When his shaking sobs subsided, he fell into sleep.

"Cry, young man. Even in your sleep, your tears promise healing. You are not fighting this alone. God is helping you."

"'*Unto Thee will I cry, O Lord, my rock; be not silent to me; lest if Thou be silent to me, I become like them that are thrown into the pit…*' That is your fear, Rudolf. God will not let go of you. 'I am alive because God willed it so'. When you feel the hand of the tempter on your heart, it will help you. '*Wait on the Lord; be of good courage, and He shall strengthen thine heart.*' God will work this in His time; you must – we all must – simply wait."

When Rudolf finally slept, Youhanna went out to the ledge to meditate. Above him stretched the Milky Way holding fast the edges of the night. Orion was bright above, the colors of its stars clear and unsullied by any earthly thing. "Such is your purity, O my Lord," said Youhanna. "The unfathomed purity of silence and dark; the windows in Heaven." He composed himself and began reciting a psalm, his promise to Rudolf, his prayer, a resolution between himself and the rocks and sky with which he lived.

"'*He that dwelleth in the secret place of the most High shall abide under the shadow of the Almighty. I will say of the Lord, He is my refuge and my fortress: my God; in Him will I trust. Surely He shall deliver thee from the snare of the fowler, and from the noisome pestilence. He shall cover thee with his feathers, and under His wings shalt thou trust: His truth shall be thy shield and buckler. Thou shalt not be afraid for the terror by night; nor for the arrow that flieth by day... There shall no evil befall thee, for He shall give His angels charge over thee, to keep thee in all thy ways. They shall bear thee up in their hands...*'."

Chapter 15, Maronites

The Crusades had brought the Maronite brethren of the Qaddisha Valley closer to the Roman church. Many had fought beside the crusaders. Some went to Rome to study, to advance their faith and legitimize their sect, which historically had adhered to the heresy that said: Christ had no human nature, only divine nature; that his will was pure divine will. The Roman church had long determined (after much bloodshed) that Christ had two natures – Divine and Human, and that in Christ they worked in concord.

The Maronite doctrine was first deemed heresy because it seemed to deny that Christ's temptation in the desert was real temptation, or so the Maronite doctrine was understood in Rome. The brotherhood explained that no, the temptation was real enough, but that Christ, knowing what he must do and would do, had in front of him at all times the Truth. "For this he is a light to us," was the explanation. "He showed us in our blindness what we must do; cleave to solitude, to silence, to God and to help one another. He showed us how man would be had he not disobeyed God." Finally, the Pope decided there was no heresy, just different language, and the two churches united.

Youhanna thought such debates were foolish. God spoke for Himself constantly. Why did men need to debate anything? "We have only to wonder. But," sighed the old man, "that may not be all that is asked of us." More *had* been asked of Youhanna. Rudolf's arrival was God's demand that Youhanna translate the truth of silence into meaning, comfort and help for this lost boy.

The morning he had looked down from the ledge outside his cave and had seen Rudolf, face down, several hundred feet below, Youhanna knew the challenge this other person would present to his relationship with God. Without thinking twice, Youhanna had abandoned the solitude in which he knew Truth, to take the hand of a fallen brother and lift him back to life. It was God's hand reaching into the life of a man.

Youhanna had stripped from Rudolf what remained of his blood and dirt encrusted clothing. "Ah," he said to Rudolf, "I read your history here." At first Youhanna thought Rudolf had broken bones in his leg, but instead it proved to be an infected wound. An arrow he had somehow removed? Or the puncture of a knife? Probably not even Rudolf knew. Youhanna cleaned the opening with a poker, red hot from the fire, and then flushed the wound with boiling water and wine. Though Rudolf felt in his flesh the sensation of pain, his mind in its oblivion registered nothing.

"Be grateful, young man, at what God is doing to save your life and, God willing, your leg," said Youhanna. "Though you do not hear me now, when you awaken, as God-willing you shall, we can talk and you can tell me what happened to you." Youhanna cleaned Rudolf's flesh from head to toe as he searched for other injuries. He found nothing beyond abrasions where Rudolf had fallen on the sand. "These are fresh," Youhanna said. "You must have fallen often on the last part of your journey, risen, and struggled on before the pain in your leg pulled you to the ground or the stream called out to you to drink."

He wrapped Rudolf's leg in strips of clean linen, then dressed him in a simple cassock. "All right, then. Sleep. Tomorrow we will know whether you will make it or not." Youhanna left him and went down to the valley to work.

***

"Look at the world around you, the world God made, not the world man has made. Look within, in the silence of this cave and the darkness of your heart. Find the reflection of that world. Look within without flinching. You will find that everything you seek is all around you, inside and out."

Rudolf's heart began to pound with fear more profound than he had felt riding into battle. He feared to look where Youhanna instructed him. To see the horrible ugliness of his own heart and soul? To look straight at the mistakes he'd made and his innumerable unknown sins?

"I am afraid," he whispered.

"That is the fear of God, my friend. You are afraid of your own heart. Some, looking upward at the night sky, feel dread. You, looking inward, believe you look into the abyss of night. Imagine, in turning there, you find God's love. What will you say then, discovering that all along He has been waiting for you to have that much courage? And that your loneliness is just the face of your fear?"

"How do you know?" Rudolf was shaking, shivering. "Have you felt this?"

Youhanna smiled gently and shook his head. "No, thanks be to God. I was born with a different temper. Still, to feel forsaken by God is not strange when the world makes no sense and we lose what we love. It is easy to forget God's mercy."

"Mercy?"

"Mercy."

"There was no mercy on that battlefield, Brother Youhanna. I gave none myself and God spared no one."

"God's mercy has nothing to do with a battlefield. Perhaps his act of mercy on behalf of mankind was sparing your life."

Rudolf shook his head.

"*'Like as a father pitieth his children, so the Lord pitieth them that fear Him. For He knoweth our frame; He remembereth that we are dust. As for man, his days are as grass: as a flower of the field, so he flourisheth. For the wind passeth over it and it is gone: and the place thereof shall know it no more. But the mercy of the Lord is from everlasting to everlasting'.*"

***

"I must leave you for two days. Will you manage?"

Rudolf looked at Youhanna, his face a question.

"The brethren in the Valley do not know you are here; it is my duty to tell them. Someone might be looking for you."

"I will go with you."

"You would not make it."

"I can try."

"Stay and care for the grapes. If you think of what you have seen and lost, talk to our Heavenly Father."

When Rudolf awakened alone in the cave the next morning, he followed Youhanna's ritual, as if otherwise the mountains and rocks would feel the loss of that spirit.

* * *

The cedars, already fully grown in Christ's time, were living green against the pale rock, rose-colored in the dawn. Youhanna took the switchbacks down the mountain in long, comfortable strides, feeling the power of his own body. Without it, he could not move, could not choose, could not seek and could not find God. Still this very tool of motion and choice posed the greatest danger. God's world was a prayer and human life the instrument, the sacrifice, the offering, yet such a problem to man.

At the bottom, where the stream and valley were widest, there was a church and a cluster of stone and mud dwellings where those who had chosen a communal life lived and kept silence together. Such was the ideal. In reality, there was often an undercurrent of disagreement, the natural result of individuals living together.

They considered Youhanna a wise and holy man, and he was much loved. He was unfailingly gentle; his compassion seemed without bottom, and he strove to listen, then to act. He avoided arguments, saying only, "It is not what we think that matters most. To learn what God thinks, we must pray and wait."

It was natural that when the residents saw the lean and ragged man enter the community, they wondered what had happened. "Brother Youhanna," said one elderly priest, approaching him with his hands held before him in the position of prayer and of blessing, signing his questions, knowing of Youhanna's vow of perpetual silence, not knowing Youhanna had been called to break that vow. "What brings you? Are you well?"

"Thanks be to God, I am well," Youhanna spoke. "I must speak with the bishop."

"Come with me. He is in the refectory right now, talking with the cooks about the Advent menu."

"I will be back," the bishop signed to the cook. "Brother Youhanna! What has happened? Are you well?"

"Yes, thanks be to God, Holy Father. I seek your counsel."

"We can talk in my rooms. We will have some privacy there." Hearing Youhanna speak, the bishop knew something very grave, very serious, had happened.

"A young man appeared in the valley weeks ago, badly injured. Have you heard of a battle?"

"Nothing nearby," said the bishop. "The loss of Jerusalem and the defeat of the Christians on that strip near Harbiyah. Could he have been caught in a raid?"

"No. A battle."

"You say he is hurt?"

"He had a badly infected wound. When I found him, he was out of his mind with fever. For some days, I wondered if the leg would not need to be cut. I did all I knew and with God's mercy won over the infection. It is not his leg that concerns me now. It is his soul. He is in great pain; grief fills his heart and mind, grief beyond the loss of his brother, who he lost in the battle. His grief seems to be knit together with his very breath. He holds himself responsible for everything."

"We find relief in our Blessed Savior from the burden of our delusions."

"Yes, Father, this I know. He also knows."

"Have you talked?"

"Often. In some way this troubles me."

"Do you want to bring him here to us? Would that relieve you? It would allow you to return to your own ways."

"I have thought about this, Father, and prayed. I will accept what God has sent. Did not our Blessed Savior say in his instruction to his disciples, 'Heal the sick, cleanse the lepers, raise the dead, cast out devils: freely ye have received, freely give'?"

The bishop saw in Youhanna's eyes all of the love and compassion a man can feel for another man. This stray and wounded straggler had further opened the heart of this most holy of hermits. Youhanna's age was clearly marked on his lean features. Were there to be a follower of this man, a student of his wisdom and ways, he would need to appear soon. Perhaps the Lord had sent Rudolf that Youhanna could teach him. The bishop looked again into the hermit's eyes, this time searching for signs of death. But Youhanna's eyes remained the eyes of youth set within the frame of passing time. "Where is he from?"

"Over the sea. The battle you have just told me about is the battle he survived."

"Survived?"

"He told me all were dead, save him."

The bishop nodded. "The news I have came to me through travelers coming up the valley toward Damascus. There were survivors, though few. They say the leader of the Hospitallers was taken captive and is held now in Cairo. This was the work of Khwaresmians and Mamluks in the service of as-Salih Ayyub."

"This is a new danger, I fear," said Youhanna, shaking his head. "Such a battle and such losses cannot…" He shook his head harder. This was not for him to consider.

"Peace, brother," said the bishop, making the sign of the cross.

"Thank you, Father."

The danger, of course, was that someone would look for Rudolf; the enemy would want to annihilate all of them or take him hostage. If he were important enough, that could be the case.

"He is not a king or the son of a king, is he?"

"Nobly born, but no. He is no danger, and if he were?" Youhanna looked suspiciously at the bishop.

"He would be safe here as long as we are safe here."

"Thank you, Father, thank you."

"Do you see him following in your path, or would his spirit benefit from the company of others?"

"I cannot tell. He has been so ill. It is difficult to separate the wounded spirit from the wounded leg and the broken heart. I pray it is only that his mind is still so close to the battlefield. When will we learn that nothing a sword can do is of any lasting value?"

"Ah," sighed the bishop. "That is the question, yet we have fought alongside them. You yourself have lifted the bow."

Youhanna nodded. "Would you confess me, Father, that I may share in the Eucharist?"

"Of course, brother," the bishop nodded.

Youhanna knelt. "Father, I beg your forgiveness and through it the forgiveness of our blessed Savior as I relate to you my many sins. Father, my most grievous sin is anger, resentment against a brother and my fear that he would disturb the tranquility of my life. I have been selfish, covetous of my relationship with God."

"Is it the boy?"

"Yes, Father. That desperate boy, in such need, and I have resented him."

"Ah, Youhanna. God tests us all." The bishop wondered what penance he could give this man who walked barefoot on rocks that steamed summer heat. Who in solitude had carved a garden from a desert of thorns. Who for years had lived in profound loneliness except for the companionship of God, the rising sun and the night sky. This man who, in imitation of St. Maron, slept outdoors in all seasons, uncovered and unprotected. Of his own accord, Youhanna would scourge his flesh for the sins he committed, the bishop knew. He yearned to say, *I have no penance for you, Brother Youhanna.* But that would make it seem to Youhanna that his sin was beyond redemption. The bishop sighed. "Brother Youhanna, say an Our Father fifty times each day to remind you that it is God's will you do, not your own. Beyond that continue as you are. This young knight may be your penance; in him, overcome your pride. In the name of the Father, the Son and the Holy Spirit, you are forgiven,

Brother Youhanna." The bishop reached down to help the old man from the floor.

Now that Youhanna had confessed, he would keep silent until he returned to his cave to hold close the grace he experienced in the forgiveness and blessing of the bishop.

***

Youhanna did not want to enter the house of the Lord unwashed as he was, so he turned to the bathhouse where, after greeting the brothers in charge, he gestured that he would wash his feet. He was given a small brush, a towel and a vial of olive oil, then directed toward a low pool. Youhanna nodded and sat down on the edge. He put his cracked and calloused feet into the warm water, relieving them for the moment of the burden of years, of the burden of miles. He spread his toes, closed his eyes and savored the sensation. He worried. Was this pleasure more than he should feel? Was it enough to open a door to the tempter? Life with people was constantly confusing to Youhanna, even something as simple as washing his feet. At his hermitage, all he need do was put his feet into the stream and let snow melt and rain water rinse away the dust. He reached into the water and scrubbed his feet until they tingled, almost until they hurt. He pulled them from the water, dried them, then rubbed them with oil. As he did so he felt more and more uncomfortable. This was enough. Vespers would be soon, and he had great need in that moment of God and solitude.

***

The Maronite order began as a loose association of hermits, but the difficulty of sustaining life in that way soon led some to form a community, keeping silence and living in poverty. Most monks lived in evangelical wandering. Their history was one of violence, persecution by pagans, infidels, and other Christian sects. They endured long stretches of famine and drought. Was God testing them? Was this God's anger? Their prayers were prayers for peace, for enough to eat, for the people to have a chance to live a full life in the service of God. As in the early days, many still lived as Youhanna did, in the rocky fastness of the mountains.

Yet, the communal rites of the church were important to all and for this Youhanna would take Mass, though to remain long with the community was impossible for him. The disputes were pits into which even the greatest soul could fall. Youhanna knew his own temper. There had been a time when he had prayed hard to discern whether it was weakness in him, or a lack of faith that made it so difficult for him to retain his connection with God when surrounded by other men. His teacher had finally resolved this for him by pointing out the differences between olives from the same tree; how some would be best eaten whole, others best crushed to oil, and others returned to the earth. "God made you like the olive to be eaten whole, Youhanna; you are not meant to mix with your brothers, pressed into oil, lost somewhere in the greater whole. Accept your nature as God's will."

* * *

A bell called out vespers and the church filled. It had been many months since Youhanna had seen so many people at one time.

Before the bishop and his assistants entered, the candles and oil lamps were lit; it was the first part of the ceremony, representing God's first creation and the coming of Christ, the light of the world, truth. An acolyte led the bishop's procession, holding a small *naqus*, two brass hemispheres on a stem, which he rang by striking them with a brass wand. The sweet pure sound signaled the presence of angels and the entry of the Holy Spirit. Two young men followed the acolyte, each swinging a brass censer.

Behind him came the choir of six monks. One carried a small hand drum, another played a stringed instrument and another played a pipe. As the bishop entered, they sang, "Make a joyful noise unto the Lord, all ye lands. Serve the Lord with gladness: come before His presence with singing. Enter into His gates with thanksgiving and into His courts with praise: be thankful unto Him and bless His name. For the Lord is good; His mercy is everlasting and His truth endureth to all generations."

In each particle of himself, Youhanna felt the beauty of voices joined in the song.

After offering a prayer for forgiveness of his own sins, the bishop spoke to the congregation. "I greet you all as we come together in fellowship to share in the miracle of Christ's resurrection through the body and blood of our Lord. Through Our Lord's compassion we are released from our sins and given eternal life, peace and forgiveness. Christ's example and His teachings show us the Holy Spirit within us and the good to which we can aspire with His help. Peace unto you."

The monks' voices reached from one side of the altar to the other. "Praise ye the Lord! From the rising of the sun unto the going down of the sun the Lord's name is to be praised. Praise ye the Lord!"

The bishop prayed, "O Lord, protect the people of the world from the scourge of wrath and protect them from dangers. Remove war, captivity, hunger and plague from us. Teach us compassion. Let us be to others as generous with our gifts as You have been to us. Help us to look beyond appearances to the soul within each man; give us the courage to reach for all who come in our way and need our help. May we be worthy to praise and confess the God of earth and sky, the Creator, the Sustainer, the Life-Giver who, in His compassion, decided to return to the heirs of Adam and pitch His tent in their midst."

Incense was burned to prepare the way for the entry of the Holy Spirit and the reading of the word of God. "Forgive us, oh Lord, our many sins."

Then a psalm was sung in preparation for the reading of the scripture. The choir began, "Blessed is he that considers the poor: the Lord will deliver him in time of trouble. The Lord will preserve him and keep him alive; and he shall be blessed on the earth."

The Holy Scripture was carried to the altar and the bishop washed his hands before touching it. "Holy Father, here we find light, and we find direction. Make us worthy of thy word, Oh Lord."

He opened the huge Bible and read, "'Master, what shall I do to inherit eternal life?' and Christ answered, 'What is written in the law? How readest thou?' 'And the answering said, 'Thou shalt love the Lord thy God with all thy heart, and with all thy soul, and with all thy strength and with all thy mind, and thy neighbor as thyself'. And our Lord said, 'Thou hast answered right: this do and thou shalt live'. He, willing to justify himself, said unto Jesus, 'And who is my neighbor?' and Jesus answering, said, 'A certain man went down from Jerusalem to Jericho and fell among thieves, which stripped him of his raiment, and wounded him, and departed, leaving him half dead. And by chance there came down a certain priest that way and when he saw him, he passed by on the other side. And likewise, a Levite, when he was at the place, came and looked on him, and passed by on the other side. But a certain Samaritan as he journeyed, came where he was; and when he saw him, he had compassion on him. And went to him, and bound up his wounds, pouring in oil and wine, and set him on his own beast, and brought him to an inn and took care of him. On the morrow, when he departed, he took out two coins and gave them to the host and said unto him, 'Take care of him, and whatsoever thou spendest more, when I come again, I will repay thee. Which now of these thinkest thou was the neighbor unto him that fell among the thieves? And he said, He that sheweth mercy on him. Then said Jesus unto him, 'Go and do thou likewise'."

Youhanna felt a surge of embarrassment. The Bishop had chosen this scripture as a benediction and a lesson to remind Youhanna that compassion was the hand of God moving the hand of man to further God's work in the world, making steps toward peace.

"Beloveds," began the bishop, "this is a story that is familiar to all of us, and yet, how do we think of it? We judge the Levite and the priest harshly – certainly our Lord meant us to judge them harshly that we would do differently – but could it be that they were unable to see the suffering of the other? In their pride were they blind to their power to help? We think, in our pride, that if this were to happen to us that we would be like the Samaritan and reach into the ditch for the fallen brother. Yet, how often do we pass by the fallen brother, not even seeing he is there? It has been written, 'All come short of the kingdom of Heaven.' In their selfishness and pride, the Levite and the priest are themselves the man in the ditch, their faces turned further into the darkness of the trench. It is for men such as these – such as we – that Christ came to the world. Mankind is frail, vulnerable to Satan. Christ's message here is not only that we must help a fallen brother, but to show us how Satan has robbed us and left us lying in a ditch by the side of the road that is our life. We are Christ's fallen brothers, and He has brought us on His bosom to the inn to be cared for with no thought for the expense; He has paid all with His life.

"We must be harsh with our own sins, but we must also remember that God knows us and judges us with the compassion we should offer to others – and to ourselves. God knows our limits and the difficulty we face. That we continue, that we persevere in the direction of His will, is all He wants. We will fail, turn to him, and find His mercy even as the thief on the cross beside our Savior found the Kingdom of Heaven in his eleventh hour. Amen."

He gently closed the great book as the monks sang.

Lord, give us
A fearless heart, like that of a child,
Stay and light our way
With eternal light.

All together sang:
We give thee thanks
O our Savior,
Thou hast become man
To return us to life.
We sing the sweetest songs
To God the Father
And to the Holy Spirit
That remains in us.

Youhanna's heart felt the sweetness of fellowship with his

brothers. In these moments of candlelight, incense, voices lifted in singing the Lord's word, all striving fell away and there was nothing but the hand of God holding them in infinite compassion.

***

He set out before first light. Even in the moonless darkness, he could find the wide way to the end of this valley that would lead him to his own trail. He was halfway to the top when the sky began to lighten. He turned toward the east to greet the morning. Men and women of his faith had lived in this valley for nearly a thousand years, surviving famine, drought, and war. Through all, the valley bore no lasting traces of the struggles that destroyed men's lives and fortunes. Youhanna believed this was God's nature, so clearly seen in the unchanging, yet always changing cliffs and hills. A spring flower faded and died, only to be replaced the following spring by one just like it, and human life? The same. Vital. Leaving a seed, a piece of itself – a child, for some, knowledge or belief for others. The hermits' seed was wisdom carried through time, added to by their own lives until, at some date, perhaps not far away, knowledge perfected in the form of Christ returned.

He walked up the switchbacks leading up the mountain to a ridge overlooking his own valley. From there, Youhanna watched Rudolf carefully loosening the soil around the roots of the grapevines. The shoulder pole and pails were to one side. Rudolf worked the soil into a berm, forming a trough that would hold rain so it could soak into the earth around the roots, then poured the water slowly into the finished channel. It first remained on the surface, but as the spaces in the soil opened, the water found its way to the roots of the thirsty grapes. He covered the hollow furrow with twigs and leaves to protect the roots from frost and keep the water from evaporating too quickly.

"At this moment, you are the very soil," thought Youhanna, observing the attention and tenderness with which Rudolf worked. "You are in darkness now, but you will not remain there. The light is coming; it is opening a door; it is coming in." He was filled with love and thanked God for that gift. In love was healing. Youhanna believed there were no accidents. The intense purposefulness of everything that grew, all he cultivated, showed him that. And Rudolf? A new purpose or a completion? Youhanna did not know, but as he approached his own valley, he felt a surge of happiness and strode in free long steps down the slope. As he neared the valley floor, he began, in a clear voice, reciting from Job so he would not take Rudolf by surprise:

> " *'Where wast thou when I laid the foundations of the earth? Who laid the cornerstone thereof, when the morning stars sang together, and all the sons of God shouted for joy? Hast thou commanded the morning since thy days? By what is the light parted, which scattereth the east wind upon the earth? Who hath divided a water course for the overflowing of waters, or a way for the lightning of thunder; to cause it to rain on the earth, where no man is; on the wilderness, to satisfy the desolate and waste ground, and to cause the bud of the tender herb to spring forth? Whose house have I made the wilderness, and the barren land his dwellings? He scorneth the multitude of the city, neither regardeth the crying of the driver. The range of mountains is his pasture and he searcheth after every green thing'.*"

***

"Brother Youhanna, did those priests lie when they said my sins would be forgiven if I came to fight the infidel?"

"Lying? No, yet I doubt they spoke the truth. They spoke from their beliefs, in the limits of their understanding, but Truth is not carried on the edge of a sword."

"But if the Holy Father in Rome told them, would it not be the truth?"

Youhanna shrugged.

Rudolf never imagined that the Holy Father could speak anything other than truth. "What then?"

"Confusion. Desire. Blindness. Anger. No one is free."

"Then what is true, Brother Youhanna?"

"True or truth? That which is true is difficult enough to distinguish from lies and illusion, but it can be done. Truth? That is different. Though I have felt it, I cannot tell you what it is. For two people to share what they each know of truth is impossible. What a man sees – what a man senses – is filtered through his life, all that he knows and all he fears. Though pure, perhaps, in the moment of its being, it is never pure thereafter. Put into words it changes. Through the ears of the hearer, it changes once more. The two perhaps believe they understand each other. Of necessity they part, going different ways. Then, motivated by the same force, one attempts to destroy what the other strives to preserve. Truth is absolute and real."

The old man reached around the sinuous trunk of the grapevine. He brought forward a limb that had begun to grow crooked, crossing over other branches. He held it gently and cut it back. When he let it go, it sprang into place, giving every sign it would grow forward now that it had been relieved from the weight of its mistake. "The natural world, this living thing," he began, "we can know similarly and share. Within the most familiar is the mystery, the truth. God has used this to explain himself to man, as he did to Job. 'Where is the way where light dwelleth? And as for darkness, where is the place thereof?' God provokes the questions." Youhanna tossed the dried branches and twigs onto a skin he would tie up by the corners and carry to the cave for the fire. "And the questions show us what we do not know. Think of this, Rudolf. Why grapes?"

Rudolf shook his head. "I don't understand, Brother Youhanna."

"Think a minute. Look at this." Youhanna held an apparently dead limb between thumb and forefinger. "Does it seem remarkable to you? We have been working here for weeks, getting them ready for spring and yet what are they?"

"Grapes?"

"They seem like dead branches to me. Barren stalks, nothing. Yet, in a few months, leaves will come forth – the people will pluck some of the most tender leaves to wrap around lamb, grain and spices. Amazing!"

Rudolf nodded, but his face showed his bewilderment.

"And later, small hard grapes will appear in perfect clusters, curling tendrils above them, shaded by the leaves. And they will grow, ever more beautiful, and become wine. Wine? You can ask, 'Why wine? What miracle is this?' Is it any wonder our Lord used the grape as a way to explain man's true nature? Within each one of us is wine, pure, good wine. It takes time; it takes time and faith to find God's will for us. It can be difficult to wait; it can be frightening because we feel lost."

Rudolf looked at the rows of grapes. Youhanna saw in everything more than Rudolf imagined could be there.

"The truth is everywhere yet so difficult to see. Come. It's getting too dark to work."

Rudolf tied the firewood into a bundle and carried it up the switchbacks behind Youhanna. On the ledge, they built the fire and Youhanna hung a pot of water over it to boil. Their dinner would be tea made from the herbs all around them and grain harvested that fall mixed with raisins and milk from the three goats that wandered the hills with Youhanna.

"So, what do you think? Do you know truth now?"

"I see how each man's needs are the same. We need food and water. We need…" Rudolf shook his head. He was at a loss.

"Much. Man is a complicated creature. Not like the goats. If I whistle, they come. In all other ways, they are independent. Not so with man. God has provided for us as perfectly as He provided for the goats, yet were God to whistle, would we go to Him? No. We would ask Him what he wanted."

"I followed God in coming to the Holy Land to fight, or so I thought."

"Nothing happens without the will of God."

"That which happened on the battlefield was the will of God? Brother Youhanna, I've told you. It was evil, pure evil."

"Do you know? We have this fire to warm us, to light our faces so we can see each other. This small fire is good; a larger fire would kill us. Now, tell me if you can, the Truth of fire. Good or evil?"

Rudolf replied, "That depends on the purpose to which the fire is put."

"Fire can act on its own," said Youhanna. "If it acts on its own, would you tell me it is evil?"

Rudolf felt that he was walking in darkness. "Maybe it depends on the effect of the fire. If it is destructive, then it is evil."

"Fire can destroy that we can start anew. To improve the crops for the next year, a farmer sets fire to his field and destroys every growing thing. Is such fire destruction?"

"You say truth is not carried on the end of a sword."

"Yes."

"In a battle, do not assembled swords, lances and men act as fire and destroy everything in front of them? Afterward the bodies lie like broken and burned stubble in a field. From this is a better crop sown and reaped? Are those dead men nothing?"

Youhanna looked at the boy with concern. "It is for this Christ left with us a ceremony, symbols, that in those moments of silence, sharing the miracle of the body and blood of our Lord, we can share the Truth with another. It is reality beyond reality, beyond what we know. We go by faith in the peaceful brotherhood of others. Yet men lift swords and shed blood for that, seeking to hold Truth in the dark ravine of their understanding."

Rudolf stabbed at the fire with a stick. "I have been told many things that are true. No one would argue them."

Youhanna sighed, then laughed. "Here I am trying to share what I know is impossible. Have this conversation with God, and then you will know what I am trying to say. 'The Heavens declare the glory of God; and the firmament sheweth His handiwork. Day unto day uttereth speech and night sheweth knowledge. There is no speech nor language where their voice is not heard... The law of the Lord is perfect, converting the soul: the testimony of the Lord is sure'. It is there, Rudolf. You will learn to see it, to hear God in the silence. 'The truth of the Lord endureth forever'. Everything else is locked in time, in the trench of human life from which Christ has delivered us."

***

In February's dark fastness, Rudolf awoke to find Youhanna lying on the ledge covered by a sift of snow. It was not so cold that Youhanna had frozen to death. He had simply drifted from sleep to death as if all were one. Youhanna's life had been once concerted motion toward the side of God. Rudolf reached for the old man's cold hand and held it to his chest as the sun began to rise. "Bless the Lord, O my soul, O Lord my God…who coverest Thyself with light as with a garment: Who stretchest out the heavens like a curtain; Who layeth the beams of His chambers in the waters: Who maketh clouds His chariot: Who walketh upon the wings of the wind." Rudolf greeted the day in Youhanna's language. The morning answered in a line of golden light.

***

"This is nothing, young Rudolf," Youhanna had said, grabbing a fold of skin between thumb and forefinger. "God made us from dust, nothing more. The force that moves us is the Holy Spirit. It is written, 'God formed man of the dust of the ground and breathed into his nostrils the breath of life, and man became a living soul.' To return this to the dust from which it came is giving the earth its due. Regard it little, Rudolf. It is your servant, not your master. If your heart beats in fear, look around to see if there is an enemy; if you see none, your body is telling you the enemy is inside. Heed it, and it will help you. Indulge it, and it will destroy you."

God had simply taken back the breath that moved Youhanna, leaving behind the shape of a man. Rudolf wrapped the body in goatskins and sat down again, this time to think. What would be right? To bury him in his fields or to carry him to the community? Was there a graveyard? Without Rudolf's accidental arrival, Youhanna would most likely have died alone here. It would have been months before anyone found out. How then? Beasts would find their way to the rotting flesh and gnaw it off the bone or carry bone and flesh to their own dens. When he was found, he might be only a beast-eaten corpse.

"It is my decision," he thought. "Only what I can bear." He looked at Youhanna's thin face, the long and wispy beard, the leathery skin. He thought of how the old man had moved with swift deliberation through the hard work of his days and the delight with which he met each morning. He felt again Youhanna's hard hand on his brow, gauging his fever. "The greatest of these is compassion."

Before noon, the sun disappeared behind low-hanging gray clouds, and the north wind began steadily and intently, bringing snow. A small fire before him, sheltered from the wind by the south-facing cliff wall, Rudolf spent the day with Youhanna's body. By morning, snow covered everything, and in the pure early light, the flat flakes shimmered like jewels. Rudolf rekindled the fire and boiled water for tea. "I am sorry, Brother Youhanna," Rudolf said softly, "but I could not bear you to lie uncovered here in death." He held the cup in his hands and drank, looking at Youhanna. "Like a father pitieth his children, so the Lord pitieth them that fear Him, for he knoweth our frame; He remebereth that we are dust. As for man, his days are as grass; as a flower of the field he flourisheth. For the wind passeth over it and the place thereof shall know it no more." Rudolf knew, then, what to do. There was nothing remaining of Youhanna but that which belonged to this valley that he had cultivated and that had fed him all his life. "This part of you is this place; your very flesh is this place; you are the dust of this place." He went into the cave, got Youhanna's shovel and went down the switchbacks to the field. Where the snow had blown away, he saw tiny shoots, the beginning of the first crop that took what it could from the winter moisture to ripen by early summer.

***

Rudolf had helped Youhanna prepare the earth for these infant plants. Each turn of Youhanna's small hand plough had revealed beneath the silty, dried clay and sand, soil that was nourishing and rich, from which grain would grow. Rudolf had followed with a hoe, breaking up the clods. The Maronites had brought life to the

Qaddisha valley, and in early times, as food had sprung from the desert, the tribesmen of the hills believed the valley held sacred healing powers because of the blessings of the Christian hermits who cultivated it. They came in their own desperate times to grab a handful of dirt with which to restore a dying child to health. In doing this, the unconverted sought conversion, bringing many more to Christ.

"It has never been the soil," Youhanna had told him. "It is only that they believe it is the soil."

"What is it then?"

"It is their faith; God's will; perhaps it is only that they try, perhaps it is because they realize that there is no hope other than in God. You see, when Father Maron arrived here, this was a barren waste. That it became what it is, a valley of wine, oil, honey, fruit and grain, seems a miracle -- is a miracle. God made this land to feed and clothe us; if tended properly, it fulfills itself. Man suffers, is ill and without hope, lives without truth, but like the land, if tended properly, each man will fulfill God's will for him."

***

Rudolf dug the grave in soft ground on the edge of the field that opened to the shovel as if to welcome the man who had loved it. The sun was high when the hole was deep, wide and long enough. "Now," whispered Rudolf, and he leaned the shovel against an olive tree. He went back up the stony switchbacks to the ledge. He crouched down, lifted the gaunt old man in his arms, and slung the corpse over his shoulder. The burden made his strides all the more unsteady.

Not long before, Youhanna had carried him up this very trail with the hope of saving his life, and now he, alive, carried what remained of Youhanna to the valley where he had himself been found. Rudolf's heart felt it would explode from the volatile mixture of wonderment and sorrow. "I did not even want this life," Rudolf said, "but you held onto it for me against the day I would see its value." The same doubt clawed at his mind and soul, but now he had weapons. The first weapon was work; the second, patience; the third, the Psalter, a font of words that through all his life he would know in Youhanna's language. Most important among them were the words, "Wait on the Lord."

Reaching the grave, Rudolf carefully shifted the corpse so he held it in both arms, face up, and as gently as possible, he dropped it into the grave. He knelt down and looked at Youhanna, knowing it would be the last time. He was shaken by the coldness inside his heart. "Old man, you saved my life, though I would have preferred to die. Now you no longer want anything. You said my life would answer my questions and would lead me to truth."

"Truth? Go to God. You will find it there," Youhanna had said.

Rudolf had shaken his head. "I went to God," he had told Youhanna, "and there was nothing there."

"My dear boy," said Youhanna, "then you did not go to God. If you had, you would have found everything."

He pushed the shovel into the pile of dirt and began filling the hole. He worked without thinking about what he was doing, but when he looked down and saw Youhanna's face nearly covered with dirt, his stomach lurched in a spasm of nausea mixed with a sudden burst of grief.

"This is nothing," Youhanna had told him, speaking of the body, "nothing."

"Yet, you saved mine. Why, if it is nothing? I don't want it."

"That which is within belongs to God. You arrived here for God's reasons. The discovery of our own purpose within God's plan is the *why* of life. 'Bless the Lord, O my soul; and all that is within me, bless His holy name. Bless the Lord, O my soul, and forget not all His benefits, who forgiveth all thine iniquities; who healeth all thy diseases, who redeemeth thy life from destruction; who crowneth thee with loving kindness and tender mercies, who satisfieth thy mouth with good things so that thy youth is renewed like the eagles.' So it is with you, Rudolf."

Rudolf shoveled through tears, no longer cold-hearted and numb. When the hole was filled, he searched for rocks to pile on the mound to keep the jackals away. When he finished, Venus was above the horizon. "I hope this is what you would have asked me to do, Brother," Rudolf said aloud to the pile of rocks. He was exhausted, mind, body and soul, as he went back up the switchbacks. He fell face down on the goatskins, asleep within minutes.

Chapter 16, Community

Without Youhanna, life was very different; the silence was absolute in this snow-muffled world. Rudolf's thoughts remained within him, seeking expression and finding no place to go. Could he remain here, carrying on for Youhanna? Tending the grapes, the olives, the grain, alone? He doubted it. Youhanna's life was a constant conversation with God. Rudolf's life would be silent. He was no ascetic; he had learned this, and though he had grown to love the grapes that were his responsibility, he felt none of Youhanna's mystical fascination for nature. Rudolf could see the hand of God but only as one might recognize the power of a great artist. The day Rudolf buried Youhanna was the one break in a weeklong storm.

He decided to leave when the storm ended. He prepared a bundle -- goatskins to keep him warm, a water bag, food and a skin of wine he would mix with water along the way, wherever the way was. He knew he had to tell the community about Youhanna's death, but after that, he did not know. He did not even think of home; he was in the world and of the world now.

He set the cave in order, leaving a pile of dried wood and kindling in a sheltered corner for whoever came next. On the first clear morning, he headed down. He walked with a limp but no crutch. His strides were uneven but long, even through drifts, and he made good speed, arriving in the early afternoon.

***

When Rudolf walked into the community, he took the monks by surprise. Rudolf had no idea where to go or to whom he should speak. The monks who saw him ran quickly to the bishop, and in complicated signs, explained that someone had arrived from outside, a young man. The bishop realized instantly who it was and what must have happened to bring him here. He signed to a monk to take

Rudolf to his chambers. He knelt, asking God's forgiveness for breaking his vow of silence during this time of day, and hurried to Rudolf. Rudolf stood before a window, looking toward the church. The bishop addressed Rudolf in perfect Latin, and, without thinking, Rudolf answered him in German, momentarily confused by the bewildered look on the bishop's face.

"Forgive me, Father. I have not heard the Latin tongue spoken so easily in a very long time." As Rudolf had learned Youhanna's own language, Youhanna had stopped speaking Latin except for short sections of a very few of the psalms he recited. "Brother Youhanna is dead."

"When?"

"A week ago. In his sleep. I awoke and found him dead."

"Where is the body?"

"I buried it on the edge of the field of grain, near the olive trees."

"He would have wanted it so," nodded the bishop.

Rudolf's eyes filled. It was nothing the bishop said, but the way in which he spoke of Youhanna, with knowledge that confirmed his own.

"It is not easy for anyone to live as Youhanna lived, that is certain. It is not within my abilities, though I lived so for a period, awaiting the Lord's direction."

"Did God send you here?" asked Rudolf.

The bishop shook his head. "He sent me to the north, to a people who had not heard of Him. I lived there for several years."

"Then?"

"I returned here. I did not again seek the solitude of the hills, but Brother Youhanna!" the bishop sighed deeply. "Never have I seen so much joy in any pair of eyes as I saw in the eyes of Brother Youhanna. Every movement of that man's life was a prayer. Will you stay here, or will you go home?"

Rudolf shook his head. "I don't know."

"Stay the winter. Many people come through, caravans and

armies both. Perhaps in one of them, you will find companions. Study here with us for a time. Perhaps our life will suit you. Perhaps in the meantime you will find you wish to return to the hills."

Rudolf nodded. He had nowhere to go and nothing within but questions.

Chapter 17, St. Augustine

"Oh God, hope of my youth, where were you all this time? Where were You hiding from me? ...I was walking on a treacherous path, in darkness. I was looking for You outside myself and I did not find the God of my own heart. I had reached the depths of the ocean. I had lost all faith and was in despair of finding the truth." St. Augustine, Confessions

The bishop's long beard was more gray than black; his hands were spotted and gnarled from time, work and sun. "I can count on one hand the times I heard Brother Youhanna's voice before he came to tell me about you. He was like his own vines, faithful to God and to the promptings of his soul."

Rudolf nodded. "Youhanna said we find within our own nature the path God has made for us. And then it is for us to decide to follow it."

"He makes it sound simple, but it is difficult in this confusing world. There is so much to draw us into illusion."

Rudolf only then thought to truly wonder where he was. Youhanna had never explained this to him. "Father, what Brethren are you?"

"We follow Jesus Christ through the teachings of Saint Maron."

"St. Maron?"

"You would not know of him," said the bishop. "We follow him as he followed Christ. According to our vows, we strive in our Lord's name to help others, to heal their diseases and to reach for them in their darkness, help them escape the snares of Satan moving endlessly around our feet, reaching for our hearts. As our Lord instructed his own followers, we leave behind home and family, wealth and attachments on earth to go into the world and tell others.

When we return, some of us serve in the community or live, as did Youhanna, alone with God. Look around the sides of the cliffs; you will see many hermit cells."

Coming down the mountain, Rudolf had noticed the windows and bricked walls high on cliff sides, elaborate compared with Youhanna's simple cave. "Why did Youhanna live so far away from the rest of you?"

"Apart from us, alone with his trees, vines, and grain, he lived in peace; the closer he got to human settlements, the farther he felt from God. He feared it was a weakness in his faith that he could not hold fast when surrounded by men. In time, he accepted that was how God had made him. But, on seeing you, he never looked back. I told him to bring you here so that he could return to his life of holy silence but he said, simply, 'Did not our Lord tell us to heal the sick, cleanse the lepers, cast out devils? 'Freely ye have received, freely give,' He said. "Now," the bishop went on, "show me that wound."

"He saved my life," said Rudolf in a flat voice. "And I did not even want it. He said that my life belonged to God, not to me, and to take something from God is to give it to Satan." Rudolf lifted the hem of his cassock until the bishop could see the still raw scar on his thigh. The bishop bent down for a closer look.

"May I?" he asked Rudolf, his fingers above the edges of the scar. "Brother Youhanna was not a bad doctor. You were fortunate to land in that valley." He hoped to get Rudolf to talk about his experience. "Does it still hurt you?" The bishop probed the edges with his thumb and forefinger. "It's healed well; there are a few places where the tissue is knotted within, but for the most part, it is even and smooth. What happened? Do you know exactly?"

"It was in battle. Swords rose and fell like hungry birds. I kept my horse longer than others. Youhanna thought it was a Khwaresmian knife that jabbed into my leg when I was still on horseback, jabbed and turned."

Rudolf spoke with no trace of sorrow or fear, as if the battle had happened to someone else or so long ago that it was only the idea of a memory.

"You lost your brother?"

"Conrad. For that God can never forgive me."

"Forgiveness is yours for the asking, even if you held the knife that killed your brother. Did you? In some blind accident on the battlefield, did your sword find the neck of your brother instead of the neck of the enemy?"

Rudolf had not thought of this possibility, and it shook him deeply. He closed his eyes, and for the first time, tried to remember the battle exactly. No. That could not have happened. Conrad had ridden ahead of him and to the right, following von Schnabelberg. Rudolf had begun in the same direction, but had suddenly found himself surrounded by Ayyubid allies in retreat from the Khwaresmians. He had stood firm where he was, turning his horse this way and that, evading the terror of the Bedouin in flight. When they had passed he awoke as from a dream and saw himself lifting and dropping his sword against this and then that wild neck. The enemy fell, one and then another, as he pressed forward, cutting through them, watching them fall as grass before a scythe.

"No, I did not kill my brother in that way. He was in front of me in battle. It is not that. It is this. He followed me away from home, and that is the same as if I killed him with my own sword."

The bishop saw the place of pain where guilt had replaced truth.

"Will you stay with us? At least until you know where you want to go?"

Rudolf, who had held his bundle on his shoulder until that moment, let it drop to the floor of the bishop's chamber, and suddenly felt the burden of all his experience. Having spoken in a language he had spoken all his life, reality seemed closer, less dreamlike than had the months on Youhanna's ledge, the psalms in the vineyard, the gentle speaking of the hermit who had so hoped with his faith to knit together Rudolf's soul. Rudolf retained the numbness of defense, but the tight chambers of his heart had opened.

Thank you, Lord, the bishop prayed silently. *None but*

Youhanna could have accomplished so much, and now? Now help me.

***

"I have something for you to do," said the bishop the next morning after breakfast. "Come with me." Rudolf had noticed a rectangular wing launching itself from one side of the chapel; this was the library. The bishop knocked softly. "Brother Stefano may be here already. He is our librarian and our scribe."

The door was opened by a very young monk; his face showed no sign yet even of a beard. "Brother Stefano, this is Brother Rudolf." The bishop looked at Rudolf, who wore the robes of the Maronites but without any religious ornamentation, no cross, nothing to mark him as one who had embraced their faith, or any faith at all. "He was, as you probably know, with Brother Youhanna for some months. Now he will stay with us at least until the end of winter. I thought he would gain some good from our library, and I would introduce him to your good friend."

The boy smiled. "With great pleasure, Father."

Rudolf was confused. What friend? There was no one in the library. It was a plain room with thick walls and windows through which the morning light spilled onto the lecterns arranged to capture the best light for reading and for transcription.

"Come in," said Brother Stefano. "You are most welcome."

The room smelled of ink, parchment, glue and incense.

"What do you think, Brother Stefano? The *Confessions?*

Stefano looked at Rudolf with a quick searching glance and nodded. He went to a chest and unlocked the lid. He withdrew a small volume wrapped in purple silk. He brought it, still wrapped, to the lectern where Rudolf and the bishop waited. He then went to a stand beside the door and filled a basin he brought over to Rudolf and the bishop. He washed and dried his hands with great care and then he unwrapped the book. It was a small volume, bound in goatskin with silver covers into which had been pressed an intricate design. In the center of the front cover was an enameled picture of a

169

man sitting, facing a woman. It could have been taken as a depiction of Christ and the Holy Virgin, but it was Augustine and his mother.

"I wonder, Rudolf, how is your penmanship? Could you copy this book for us? This one is quite old, very fragile, one of the oldest in our small collection. It is one of the most often read. I fear its destruction through time and the many hands who touch it."

Rudolf had not imagined himself a scribe, but he thought his writing was clear enough.

"Let me write for you, Father, and you decide."

Stefano placed some ruled parchment in front of Rudolf with a quill and ink. Rudolf washed his hands and dried them on the towel Stefano held out for him. "What shall I write, Father?"

The bishop paused only a second, "For God so loved the world..."

Rudolf nodded, and drawing his long sleeve back from his right hand, he picked up the pen and dipped it into the ink, allowing a stray extra drop to fall back into the well. With no little grace, Rudolf lay down the strokes of a larger initial letter and followed that with the well-known verse in a clear book-hand. When he finished, he poured fine clean sand over the surface to dry it, protecting it from smearing, and handed it to the bishop.

"Well," said the bishop, "it is clear and even, very readable. This will not be a fancy volume, perhaps no ornamentation at all, but one that will serve those who need to read the story the Blessed Bishop has told. "Do you know this work, Rudolf?"

"No, Father. All I know is the *Rule*."

Rudolf copied from the *Confessions* every morning. In this way, in this small bright room, Rudolf met the teacher who would inform his life. St. Augustine's desperate seeking gave Rudolf's searching heart a companion. Augustine's rational mind and soul-filled determination prepared a road to the answers Rudolf had longed for, a man in direct conversation with Christ, far from the half-superstitious black and white doctrine of the Black Robes or his mother. This man had asked Rudolf's own questions, stumbled in the same darkness, felt the same despair.

It was not a first meeting. This was the same mind behind the *Rule* that governed the knightly orders, and Rudolf knew the *Rule* in and out; he had used it over and over to give direction to his wandering heart.

Augustine, too, wanted proof of the existence of God, and in this determination, had wandered far from the religion in which he had been raised only to discover that every proof was subject to disproof and argument. Truth had to be beyond proof. His own reasoning mind told him that. On this Youhanna had also insisted, but his way was to look at God's creation for the hand of God within it. "It is all around you, young Rudolf," he had said. "If you catch but one glimpse of it, you will always know, and then your doubts will vanish. The apostle Paul writes of it in a letter,, 'For the invisible things of Him from the creation of the world are clearly seen'."

Rudolf had looked. He had followed Youhanna into the vineyard, into the field, onto the mountain; he had listened, looking at the night sky, to Youhanna's singing of psalms into darkness, to the pristine light of stars.

That morning Rudolf found in Augustine the words used by Youhanna to show him. "For the invisible things of him from the creation of the world are clearly seen…" These two were telling him the same thing. Augustine was not Youhanna; he was an urban cosmopolitan, a man of the senses. He struggled to decide between his love of women, one woman, and the promptings of his heart toward Christ. He wrote freely of his various lusts and confusions, seeing them as errors leading somehow to the right path. He stood at the end of his road, regarding his progress and wrote his *Confessions,* and in them, Rudolf found a light in the darkness. He followed that light when he understood fully what it had for him. When he awoke in the dark morning anxious and despairing, he quickly dressed, washed and went to the library.

As he copied, more of Augustine found its way to his heart. On reaching the ninth chapter of the *Confessions*, Rudolf was stunned to read his own questions as they had come from the pen of this other man:

> *Who am I? What kind of man am I? What evil have I not done? Or if there is evil that I have not done, what evil is there that I have not spoken? If there is any that I have not spoken, what evil is there that I have not willed to do? But You, O Lord, are good. You are merciful. You saw how deep I was sunk in death, and it was Your power that drained dry the well of corruption in the depths of my heart. And all that You asked of me was to deny my own will and accept Yours.*

"What evil have I not done?" echoed Rudolf, first in his mind and then aloud. Evil was exactly like the serpents in the desert that fated night. He closed his eyes and recalled the moment of bright moon and rising, hungry desert snakes. The image had been lost in the battle, in the death, and in his despair, but he had been given something that night he could have taken with him into battle against not only the Khwaresmians, but against despair and emptiness. He had forgotten.

Augustine wrote of the profound effect of the psalms on his tortured heart and mind, and Rudolf heard Youhanna. Others had fought for Augustine as Youhanna had fought for him. Rudolf, wondering if ever again Augustine found himself in battle against the enemy, read of Augustine's determination to begin anew, a new life as a new man, in a new faith. Augustine's resolution was fixed. The truth was no longer a riddle but a name -- Christ.

"I will do this," said Rudolf to himself. "My new name will be my sword in the sand." He finished writing the chapter and spent that afternoon in prayer, for the first time abandoning himself and all of his questions to silence. He left them behind him to spin like sand in the corners of the sanctuary, and he went in search of the bishop. "Holy Father, can I speak with you?"

"What is on your mind?"

"I wish to be re-baptized. I would like a new name to fit the man I am now."

The bishop nodded.

"So much has happened. I am still filled with doubt, but now I know that doubt does not lead to answers. Faith does. I am not the only one to doubt."

"By no means," said the bishop, smiling.

"In St. Augustine I have found an ally, a friend."

"It is for this he is so well-loved. He is a man with a human heart, who sought God with that heart, answering the voice of God within him. Do you wish to take the name of Augustine?"

"No." Rudolf felt a lump rise to his throat. "I wish to take the name Youhanna."

"Youhanna?"

"Yes. He saved my life. He showed me the night sky, the pathway to the Truth. He sacrificed his own peace for my life and the possibility that within this," Rudolf thumped the space above his heart with his fist, "lay a soul that God could love. He was what Augustine has written about, the charity that is truth. If I can be somehow in this world what Youhanna was in my world, I will have done well with the gifts God has given me."

The bishop was moved. "And then? Will you return to Youhanna's cave and follow his way?"

Rudolf shook his head. "It is not my way. I will take Youhanna with me into the world and try to live the charity that Youhanna lived with me. I have seen suffering with war. Even without war, men suffer. Had Youhanna not saved this simple animal thing," Rudolf pinched the skin of his own cheek above his beard, "I would have died. I would not have learned what I have learned and though the darkness may come upon me again, I now have something with which to resist Satan's cold hand. Youhanna gave me my life."

The last Sunday before Lent, Rudolf was baptized and the name Johannes was added to his own. Immediately after, partly to contemplate in solitude the great changes within him but also to see how things fared in Youhanna's valley, Rudolf returned alone to the cave. Spring had reached the valleys. The mulberries and grapes would be, at the very least, in bloom if not already setting on with fruit. He imagined how the grain might have grown; he wondered about the olive trees, if all was well, or if wanderers or beasts had disturbed the valley. As he made his way over the ridge from which Youhanna had watched him at work irrigating the grapes, he stopped. The view made his heart ache. He felt the absence of the man for whom it had been home. "I have taken your name, old man," he said aloud to the olives, the grapes, the grain. He loped down the hill to the valley floor. He heard a wild hum of bees; the world, which had been snow-covered and asleep, was awake, pushing toward hope, expectant. On the way up the hill to the cave, he went through the vineyard. "…in a few months, leaves will come forth – the people will pluck some of the most tender leaves to wrap around lamb, grain and spices. Is that not amazing?" And here it was.

***

When Rudolf returned to the community three months later, he found the church and library had been sacked and burned. There were no new graves, so Rudolf knew the monks had been warned and had had time to flee. But where? He wandered through the ruins, his heart too empty for despair. Outside the burnt library he kicked up a Khwaresmian knife. Not knowing what lay ahead, he put the weapon into his belt before turning to the road that led west to the port city of Beirut. He would return to Europe wearing the robes of a Maronite monk and carrying *The Confessions of St. Augustine* copied in his own hand.

Chapter 18, Modona

"It doesn't matter. Good or evil, the result is the same. We are here now. Our struggle is against sin. Man is evil or there would be no struggle. We would be one with God." In lisping Spanish Latin, the Dominican friar disputed furiously with a much younger Franciscan.

"What of the impulse toward good given us by our Heavenly Father in whose image we are made?" The young Franciscan's voice had barely broken.

Though Rudolf listened, he wanted very much to sleep.

"Free will leads us away from God, over and over again. Can you argue that this does not say something about the evil nature of man?"

Their voices rose, louder, more emphatic, more excited. The voice of the Franciscan began to crack, wavering between manhood and boyhood. He was outmatched.

"If our nature were so hopeless, would our Heavenly Father have sent his Son? There would have been no question even then of our redemption, but our Lord Jesus Christ did come and give himself for the redemption of our iniquity. We are returned – all of us – to the blessed state before the fall!" The young Franciscan was adamant in his sweet hopefulness.

"It is BECAUSE man's nature is hopeless that Our Heavenly Father sent his son. We are no different from Adam. We make the same defiant choices. You talk as if there were no Tempter."

"Quiet! You're keeping us awake! We'll find out soon enough, but right now I wish you both would go to the Devil." The angry shipmate crossed himself.

"He's right," thought Rudolf, who lay in the shadows of the deck like the others, trying to sleep.

"We will be in Modona tomorrow. You can take your arguments off the boat," a passenger added, rising slightly to adjust his clothing bundle for a better pillow.

Rudolf smiled at the Franciscan who lay beside him, and said gently, "Sleep may be a better way to pass the time." Part of him wished to tell this young man of Youhanna, and of Youhanna's belief that such discussions led men away from God, but by doing so he would himself enter this futile and increasingly angry dispute.

***

The boat tacked from side to side on calm seas as it neared the fortified port of Modona. Rudolf had no idea where he would go next. There were ships to all ports leaving from this Venetian fortress, this Grecian city. He had traveled from Sidon as a pilgrim. Giving passage to pilgrims returning from Jerusalem brought the captain a few steps nearer Heaven, and if the ship were not heavily loaded with items for trade, extra passengers provided ballast in a strong wind.

"Join us in Assisi," whispered the young monk to Rudolf.

Rudolf shook his head. "No, I need to go home."

"We are a peaceful brotherhood."

"I do not have a peaceful heart."

"What will you do then?"

"I don't know. Sleep." Youhanna had taught him how wounds were to be healed rather than inflicted; if others must fight for God in that way, let them. First, he would heal the wounds he inflicted on his family, on Gretchen, if he could. Then? He did not know other than he would not lure young men to battle with promises of salvation or argue with anyone about the meaning of God's word.

The moment he had seen the ruins of the Maronite community, he had wanted to pick up a sword, to find a horse, to pursue those who had destroyed everything, to slaughter them in the same wild violence. He had become somehow a military man. Turning the other cheek was not his nature. The pacifism of his early youth had been only the inertia of melancholy.

"I love peace," he had told the young friar earlier, "but in no peaceful way."

"Peace is God's way," the Franciscan insisted.

Rudolf looked into the young man's soft brown eyes. "Perhaps, but peace is not the nature of this world." He was thinking of St. Augustine's words, "'...for the sake of peace, men fight wars'."

***

The whole wild tapestry of humanity in transit engulfed Rudolf and his young companion the moment they disembarked in Modona. Now in the control of the powerful city-state of Venice, the port was so crowded with refugees from the Holy Land, pilgrims, members of the brotherhoods, as well as merchants from everywhere, priests and monks, thieves, whores and con men, that Rudolf could barely move. Beggars plucked at their sleeves. The Franciscan was soon lost in the press of people searching for each other, searching for their things, searching for a way out. Rudolf decided to find passage to Venice and to get away from there, but before he could escape the crowd, he was grabbed by a ragged old woman, her neck strung with glass beads, a gold ring in one ear.

"Come with me, come with me. I will tell your future, young lord. I can tell you now, it is a good future, a bright future, a happy home, wife, children -- all sons! A very long life."

"Impossible." He felt his life had been very long already.

"A coin then, for the moment of hope?"

"Hope?" thought Rudolf. Hope was the partner of desire and he had none. There was nowhere he wanted to go, nothing he wanted. He only went where he had to go. He gave her a few pennies and shook free of her brown, bony hand, and pushed his way through the crowd. Anyone else would want that fortune.

Ships and boats filled rapidly, following the immutable laws of supply and demand, and passage was expensive. Returning warriors were given preference, but there was nothing in Rudolf's appearance that showed he was a Teutonic Knight. He wore the robes of a

Maronite monk under his goatskin vest. Over his shoulder, he carried Youhanna's goatskin water bag, and at his waist he wore a goatskin pouch that held only his book, his few coins, and a little food.

He pushed through a crowd that was listening to a handful of Dominican Friars shouting out the Pope's call for a new Crusade. "Our Holy Father has written, 'Deeply sorrowful at the grievous dangers of the Holy Land, but especially at those that have recently happened to the faithful settled there, we seek with all our heart to free it from the hands of the wicked.'"

Rudolf knew what would come as surely as he knew anything; simple vengeance dressed in salvation's robes. These people, many fleeing raids in which they lost their homes and family, were being asked to avenge Conrad, von Schnabelberg, the rest, but it would bring no one back. It was cruel madness, which was no longer for him the inspiring call to faith.

"The Holy Father says more. 'We, therefore, trusting in the mercy of almighty God and in the authority of the blessed apostles Peter and Paul, do grant, by the power of binding and loosing that God has conferred upon us, albeit unworthy, unto all those who undertake this work in person and at their own expense, full pardon for their sins, and we promise them an increase of eternal life at the recompensing of the just.' Those who join the French King, Louis, in his campaign against the infidel can be sure that they will find eternal rest on the right hand of our Heavenly Father. Their sins, sincerely repented, shall be forgiven."

Rudolf listened. *Ah*, he thought, *the French king*.

"We must," continued the Dominican, "put aside our feuds and join against the enemies of the true God, the Evil Emperor, Friedrich, and those who support his unholy causes. The clear line of God's will and desire is the safety of the Holy Land."

A call for Crusade was not surprising, but the crowd's reaction was. Many openly mocked the friars and the Pope. "Innocent? How many offices are filled with the Pope's bastards!"

"That Roman bastard would not go," someone yelled. "So we should?"

"Who has not lost a loved one to this vain struggle?" another called out.

The crowed hurled vegetables and eggs at the black-robed monks, while others spoke out fiercely on behalf of the Emperor. The entire region had split into faction and feuding, and the splits between pro-Papal and pro-Imperial groups, private interest and family power were palpable.

"At least our Emperor made peace in Jerusalem, a peace of ten years time!"

Rudolf felt that at any moment the crowd could erupt in riot.

"And you, Brother?" asked a man standing beside Rudolf. "Would you take up the cross?"

Rudolf shook his head. "No. I will not go again and if you ask me my opinion…" Rudolf paused. Those around him had turned to listen to what he had to say.

"I ask it now. What is your opinion?" The man seemed ready for a fight, but for whose side?

"I would tell you to stay home. There is no sacrifice left for me. Though I cared little for it, I came away with my life. Now I must live that life."

"Just so," said the man, satisfied. "Just so."

"Young knight!" called a voice behind Rudolf. "Over here." The man spoke German. Hearing his own language, at once foreign and homely, Rudolf spun around to see a man in the insignia and cape of the Teutonic Knight. "Come away from this."

Rudolf threaded through the volatile crowd as quietly and invisibly as he could, guided by the voice of home. Anything could disturb the delicate equilibrium of the moment, even an accidental rough gesture from him.

The man who had spoken to him reached for Rudolf's hand. Rudolf returned the secret signs that identified him. "Come along," said the older knight, and turning forcefully but with great calm, they escaped the crowd and wandered through the narrow, labyrinthine streets, reaching, finally, the hospice and headquarters of the

Teutonic Knights. Rudolf looked around him, stunned. He had traveled so long alone on whim and desperation that he had almost forgotten his world.

"I am Brother Götz."

"Rudolf."

"Where do you come from, Rudolf?"

"Appletree Village. You?"

"Constance."

Rudolf saw a man near his father's age with, perhaps, his father's experience. His cheek wore a shallow scar. Götz caught Rudolf's eyes and said, "A knife, in the night. It was a warning, I guess. A Hospitaller blade."

Rudolf shook his head. That the Orders fought amongst themselves did as much as the infidel to destroy the Latin Kingdom of Jerusalem. "Where were you?"

"On board ship. We were young, eager for battle and so began it ourselves. It was a waste. It still is a waste. Well, Rudolf, here is the bathhouse. Bathe and I will find something for you to wear, unless you've joined the Maronites in the meantime."

Rudolf nodded. "I did."

"Then you'll go back?"

Rudolf shook his head. "There is no back."

Götz looked at him as if he would hear more, but Rudolf simply sighed, "A very long story."

"I'll go get you some clothes. We can talk later." Götz returned with the tunic and cape of the Teutonic Knights. The tunic was finer than Rudolf had ever seen, and the wool of the cape was so soft and so light it seemed too rare to warm anyone.

"What is it?"

"Wonderful, aren't they? These Venetians have built for themselves a snug little world where there is only the best of everything. The tunic is a fabric from India. They pick the floss right from a bush and spin it almost immediately into thread. The cape is from the wool of Turkish goats. Soft but very warm."

Seeing the black cross appliquéd and embroidered over his left shoulder, Rudolf braced himself for the ambush of memory, but only threadbare images of Gretchen and her mother stitching the cross on his woolen cloak wafted feebly through his mind, as dim and far away as someone else's story.

"I must take you to the Commander before vespers, but now we can talk," said Götz, leading Rudolf along an arched stone walkway toward the dormitory. "Tell me what you will. Men do not arrive at this port dressed as Maronite monks every day."

"There was a battle and most were killed, but I survived. I don't know why. Somehow I arrived in Jerusalem and left with a group of refugees. I was wounded in the battle. It's a long story, but I lost consciousness in the middle of the Maronite country and spent some time with them. Khwaresmians raided the community and wiped them out, and now I am here. That is all."

"What battle?"

"Above Gaza, perhaps three years back."

Götz nodded. "I know of only two of our brotherhood, and now, you."

Rudolf's heart beat faster in spite of himself.

"Other survivors?" He hoped but did not want to hope for Conrad, for von Schnabelberg.

"I do not know their names. I believe they are still in the Holy land. They were in Jerusalem when it was taken and had come from Starkenberg. One was captured and released. He had nothing the infidel wanted, no rich family, no large ransom, no power they could take for themselves. It was surprising that he was not killed. I understand he staggered into Baibar's camp at dusk the second day."

"Second day?"

"The battle lasted two days, I'm told. Some say it was but one."

"One unending day." Still, Rudolf felt the claw of guilt again reach toward his heart. What if? He shook the feeling away. He had been there. He walked away from a field covered with death. If there were a second day of battle, who called it? Who organized it? And who, for the love of God, fought? "Ah. I hope always to hear that my brother somehow made it out. There were not so many of us on that plain."

"You did not find his body? No, no, of course not. Such a thing is more difficult than any who have not seen such a field can imagine."

Rudolf nodded. "I walked over men and horses, parts of men, parts of horses for hours until I couldn't see anything but blood. The jackals began to gather, carrion birds swooped lower and all I thought was to get away. I wandered off that battlefield and fell into a ditch to sleep."

Götz nodded. "What will you do now?"

"I will go home."

Götz pointed Rudolf to an empty cot. Rudolf lay down and was quickly asleep. When Götz awakened him hours later, Rudolf did not know where he was. He reached for his Arab knife, but found he was unarmed.

"Rudolf, it is all right," said Götz softly. "You are in a safe place, and we have found you passage on a ship for Venice. It is leaving in an hour."

Chapter 19, Home

And, lo! My infancy died long since, and I live. St. Augustine, *Confessions*

They had meandered up the foggy lagoon to the crowded Venice harbor. Lanterns on small boats cast yellow circles on dawn's dim blue. Rudolf heard voices calling out in languages he did not know, colloquial Venetian and Slavic dialects from the mountains and forests inland from the Adriatic coast. Bells rang throughout the city, calling people to get up, to pray, to start their business. The boatman held a rope, ready to put the ship ashore.

Rudolf searched the water's edge for something resembling his memories, but there was no golden light, no misty turquoise sky, no riotous market of joyous vendors peddling untried fruit, no lascivious, dark-eyed girls stalking the wharf, hoping to tantalize the passengers as they disembarked. The dock was empty. Nor, did Rudolf think, his travel-weary, world-weary shipmates could be easily captivated. They had seen it and knew very well what they would never again see was what they had left behind. Rudolf did not yet grasp that all had changed as the world went its way. Behind the curtain of illusion waited what only experience could reveal, the human struggle to survive, hope, despair, moments of longing, love, and over all of everything, the desperate need of all living things for compassion.

The boatman tossed his rope to another who'd jumped across to the landing. Others caught the ship with hooks and pulled it to the wharf. A narrow plank was dropped onto the pier. Rudolf looped his goatskin bag over his shoulder and adjusted the Khwaresmian knife he wore on the belt around his waist. He was the first off the boat, followed soon by Herr Götz and a ragged assortment of pilgrims, refugees and tired knights. The boat carried no traders and did no trading; it simply delivered silk. Merchants dressed in lustrous furs and rich brocades stood in small black boats, waiting for their cargo.

"Come," said Götz. "Let's see if we can find a bunk." They crossed St. Mark's Square and followed a narrow street left of the huge new church with its stolen bronze horses and the pilfered bones of St. Mark. None of this figured in Rudolf's memory of Venice, which held only Conrad and his own failed vows to protect his brother from sin.

***

The Teutonic Knights maintained a hostel that welcomed the wanderers and gave them beds and food. At the evening meal, they heard news of the Crusade to the East into Prussia and Hungary. Whole villages went to settle in the conquered lands, following the knight who was their lord. It was a way to slow the embittered feuding that had erupted everywhere since the Emperor's death.

"Will you join them, then?" asked a one-eyed Brother who served their meal.

"I will," said Götz, "but my friend here? I think he has had enough of war."

"You have taken vows," exploded a burly, red-haired knight at the end of the table, looking straight at Rudolf. "They are not to be walked away from so easily."

"I am not walking away from anything. I have since taken other vows, vows to me more sacred because they do not demand I kill others for something I cannot understand."

"What vows are those?"

"Rudolf here," smiled Götz, putting his arm around the shoulders of the younger man, "has become a monk."

"So why are you not dressed as such? What right have you to wear that cape now?"

"He must wear something," said Herr Götz with a patience that won Rudolf's admiration. "We met in Modona. His monk's robes were filthy, shredded, a disgrace."

"Where did he come from?"

"The Holy Land," answered Götz. "He survived that slaughter in Gaza."

All eyes turned to Rudolf, who blushed, looked at his meal, and nodded.

"Survived? Hell's own season!" the burly knight spoke now in a hushed voice. "My apologies then, sir. I was hasty. Forgive me."

"Do not worry," said Rudolf. "It doesn't matter."

"How," asked another, crossing himself, "did you get away from that? By the grace of God, no doubt."

Rudolf nodded. "That is as unclear to me now as it was then. I came away with something I did not value, and now I must learn how to make good of it."

"What is that, young lord?"

"My life," replied Rudolf.

"Leave him," said Herr Götz. "He has lost his brother; he nearly died himself. God has cared for him in ways I can only call miraculous."

"Where will you go, then?" asked the one-eyed knight.

"Home to make things right with my mother, my father, and the girl I was to marry. Then, I do not know exactly. Somewhere I can serve God."

"Where is home?"

"North. Near Zürich."

"There has been raiding up there. I pray your people were nowhere near it."

As always, thought Rudolf. His father's holdings were small and vulnerable. Of course his father knew this and had worked hard since his return to stay out of the ever-shifting alliances and focus on his horses, but his land -- though not a large holding -- was smack in the middle of the acreage of three fiercely competing lords. Rudolf knew his marriage to Gretchen would have helped his father's security, and felt a passing, quavering guilt. Deep down he knew it would not have made much difference.

***

He set out with Götz and others, and they traveled together until they reached the River Po. From there, Rudolf turned westward on a riverboat, heading toward Milan. He did not linger in Milan, even knowing it was the home of St. Ambrose, St. Augustine's great teacher. Fighting between those loyal to the late Emperor and those loyal to the Church had made the whole of Lombardy a region to escape. He had turned his cape inside out and offered no conversation. His goatskin bag and curved knife told their own fierce, silent story.

He crossed the Gotthard Pass with a pilgrim caravan, over the narrow bridge that spanned the swollen Reuss. Once across, they all hugged the mountain walls, slow step followed by slow step so as not to be blown from the narrow ledges that traced the mountainsides. At last they descended through wild enchanted valleys into bright summer meadows and the great blue lake between the Alps. Rudolf went by pilgrim ferry from Vluolon across the lake to Luzern.

Soon he found himself on paths and roadways that carried in their ruts and resting dust memories of other journeys he had taken. Rudolf had dreaded this, that the ghost of Conrad hid at dark forest turnings, but there were only the two wheeled carts pulled by oxen, goats or mules, horsemen and wandering tradesmen as any other day in all of Rudolf's life. Perhaps he would reach home and find that he had never left.

***

He was not surprised to find Castle Lunkhofen burned. The tower his grandfather had built still stood, though the roof had fallen. Some sections of the outer wall had collapsed. Rudolf kicked through stones and cinders mixed with dirt, leaves and pine needles, finding bits of his family's life, a bronze cross, a pan, shattered crockery. A broken knife. A key. A hinge. A lock that closed a vanished book. His mother's *Lives of the Saints*? This had been Heinrich's great hall.

Wondering what happened to his father's horses, Rudolf

walked down the hill to find the stables flattened. Already grass and young poplars poked through the ash and bits of broken board. He knew then for certain that the fire had been no accident. A chill lifted the hairs on the back of his neck, ghosts passing. Rudolf drew his cloak tighter around him. To whom would he make amends now? He had felt more sorrow seeing the ruined Maronite church than he felt seeing the ruins of his childhood home. *Perhaps,* he thought, *I am the heartless wretch my mother so often said I was.* In any case, there was nothing he could do at this moment, no one he could ask.

He walked back to the ruined castle and set his bag against the highest wall. He kicked debris away from a space in front of him, finding under everything some dried leaves, sticks, and bits of cloth. Wall tapestry, altar cloth or cloak, Rudolf could not tell and did not care. He took his tinderbox from his bag and struck the flint. He slowly built up a fire until there was flame enough to keep him company as the evening mist rising from the river made the landscape as nebulous as dreams. Across Rudolf's exhausted mind floated echoes of the song that had once filled this space and sent everything in mot*ion:*

> *Alas, all my years, where have they disappeared?*
> *Have I dreamed my life, or is it real?*
> *That which I thought was something, was it something?*
> *Perhaps I have been sleeping, and do not know it.*
> *Now I am awake and all seems strange*
> *That used to be familiar, once, as my own hand*
> *The people and the place where I grew up*
> *Seem alien, like lies, not of my own land.*

Chapter 20, Morning

"Maker of all, the Lord,
And Ruler of the height,
Who, robing day in light, hast poured
Soft slumbers o'er the night,

That to our limbs the power
Of toil may be renew'd,
And hearts be rais'd that sink and cower,
And sorrows be subdu'd."

> St. Ambrose, quoted in St. Augustine's
> *Confessions,* Book 9

Rudolf awoke to the warm sunlight hitting his cloak. Accustomed to sleeping in any odd spot, he did not immediately know where he was. *More ruins*, he thought. *Another battle.*

Then he remembered. In all his wanderings, he had never felt more lost than on these still familiar hills with their forests and their apple trees. Conrad had sought change, not Rudolf, but now his own home seemed a foreign country.

"All right then," he said to himself. Standing, he shook the leaves and sticks from his cloak. *"Bless the Lord, O my soul, O Lord my God...who coverest thyself with light as with a garment: who stretchest out the heavens like a curtain; who layeth the beams of his chambers in the waters: who maketh clouds his chariot: who walketh upon the wings of the wind."*

He resolved to go down to the village for news of his family.

It was known as Apple Tree Village, this small town beside the Cistercian monastery. The apple trees grew on south facing hillsides as had Youhanna's grapes. Fallen petals still covered the ground beneath some of the trees. On others, the tiny apples had set on. Rudolf noticed how the branches of mature trees were pruned to keep the boughs from dropping heavy fruit while the young trees, for the moment, seemed to grow wild.

Conrad. Rudolf shook his head.

The monastery at the bottom of the hill would be his first stop. How would he look to the calm White Friars when he appeared in his dirty cape, his Maronite robes, his goatskin pouch, the knife at his belt? And what would he say? What did he want? He crossed himself. A whole world had run beneath his feet, a world of violent strangers and lost friends. "Thy will be done, O Lord."

The young monk who opened the door motioned Rudolf inside.

"Father Markus?" asked Rudolf, simply.

The young monk nodded and motioned Rudolf to sit on a bench in the anteroom and passed silently down the hallway leading to the church where Rudolf and Conrad had taken their vows.

Morning sunlight through colored windows brought the walls to life. The painted figures seemed to stir as the shadows from breeze-blown linden trees moved across them. Rudolf looked absently at the idealized forms of Jesus speaking with his mother, behind him a Jerusalem that resembled not at all the fetid enraged broken city Rudolf had escaped.

"Why am I here?" he asked himself. "Was there nowhere else to go?" Something grabbed his chest, the sharp claw of truth. "I still hope."

"You wanted to see me?"

Rudolf stood. The priest peered closely at his face, into his blue eyes.

"Young lord. It cannot be possible. You are home." The priest crossed himself. "Have you seen the castle? It was burned just last year. No, no. Perhaps two years ago."

Rudolf nodded. "I went there first. I slept last night in the courtyard." He did not want to ask the questions he had to ask. What of his parents? Of Gretchen?

"Your father and mother escaped, though not unharmed. Whoever burnt the castle stole your father's beautiful mares and turned the others loose. Thieves, only, or so it is believed."

Rudolf nodded. "Where are my parents?"

"With Sir Adelbert and his lady."

"You said they were hurt?"

"Your father fought for his castle and his family -- and his horses."

Rudolf hesitated, then, "And my mother?"

Rudolf shivered in pity for his mother. Still, he could imagine the reproaches heaped upon him in his absence and his father in situ.

Father Markus shook his head. "Young Lord, your father lost his sight in the fire. Your mother has lost her mind. It is well you are home. It might bring your mother's senses back to know she has not lost both sons."

"Conrad is dead," said Rudolf. "I fear she'll find me cold comfort when I tell her that."

"We believed you were dead and you are not. Perhaps..."

"Perhaps. . .," said Rudolf, shaking his head. "This is all I have, Father." Rudolf gestured at himself, his worn shoes, tattered tunic, the worn and borrowed cape of the Teutonic knights. "I have been living a vagabond life."

"You are welcome to stay here, young lord. As long as you need."

"Thank you, Father."

"Your father still has his lands, of course, but no way to care for them. One of the tenants looks after things for him and Mayor Mülner and Sir Adelbert take care of your father's business. He spoke at first about rebuilding the castle, but now, I fear, he no longer cares."

"I can well imagine. What would he build it for? Two sons who went away?"

"You had a little sister. Mathilde. She perished in the fire. Well, come on. Let's find you some clothing and a bath. Your cloak could use a cleaning as well. Then breakfast? We have already had ours but I can have a tray brought to you."

Rudolf followed Father Markus to a visitor's cell, spare and clean, with a sturdy bed, a straw mattress, a blanket. The Cross hung above it, and a table sat beside it.

"Will this be all right, young lord?"

Rudolf recalled Youhanna sleeping soundly on his ledge, of his own long night in the ditch with the dead and of the golden-lit dormitory in the Maronite Community. There was the ship, the argument between the two young priests, his many nights on the open road, last night in the ruins of his father's castle. "Oh my," he replied. "It will do very well."

***

Father Markus later found Rudolf walking in the monastery garden, reading. He looked more like the young man who had gone off with his brother for the sake of his soul, but there was no question he was older now, not only in years, but in the wisdom Father Markus had seen peering from the depths of Rudolf's blue eyes.

"Young Lord, if I am not interrupting, I would like to talk to you about your family."

"Of course, Father Markus."

"They have heard about the battle in which Lord Schnabelberg died and of the few survivors -- none now, we have heard, but William of Brienne and a priest. That you fought in that battle and did not die is a miracle."

"It did not at first feel that way. I went hoping to die."

Such a wish was a sin, and Father Markus crossed himself and then again, having had his fears confirmed.

"Our Heavenly Father was watching out for you, Young Lord."

Rudolf sighed. "All that was a long time ago."

"It was not God's will that you die. That much is clear."

"That much. I don't know what I expected in returning. I might not have, but it seemed I had to. One after another place of rest, home, was destroyed, beginning with Conrad. Everything seemed to present an argument for my return, but to what? I really never thought what. To make peace with my parents, to ask their forgiveness and to join you here and honor vows I took in a faraway brotherhood. That was, I guess, as much as I had planned. I had forgotten how life and death shake all worlds."

"Vows, young lord?"

"I am a monk. I took my vows in the Maronite community."

"Maronite?"

Rudolf nodded. "Christians living in the hills of Mt. Lebanon."

"That complicates things," Father Markus said. He had already planned Rudolf's future. He would pick up where he left off, marry Gretchen, rebuild the castle, care for his parents, and bring his own children into the world. All would be well again for Heinrich and Anna. "Life is a string of vows, is it not, young lord?"

"So it seems."

"On your journey home, had you no thought of Gretchen?"

Rudolf shook his head. "I assumed she would have married by now. I have not thought of her without thinking that it was a poor bargain to break her heart so that I could go off and watch my brother die. I sowed nothing but pain with my best intentions."

"She has not married."

Rudolf's heart leapt in spite of himself. It was an unexpected reaction.

"Her days are given to caring for your mother and father who, in spite of the arguments presented by her own mother, Gretchen views as her own parents."

Blood rushed to Rudolf's head.

"Quite naturally, the Schneebelis, Sir Adelbert and his lady, would like their daughter to marry."

Rudolf nodded. They'd had no sons. In marrying Gretchen, he would have someday become lord of Sir Adelbert's estate, Schneebeli/Lunkhofen. Another broken vow, that between Heinrich and Adelbert.

The bell rang for Vespers and the two men went in. Rudolf knelt together with the brothers in the chapel in which his life -- and Conrad's -- had been consecrated in service to God. The room, then so pale and terrifying, silver gray and filled with portents, now showed itself to be a simple chapel with a carved and painted wooden altar, an elevated pulpit and room only for 100 kneeling faithful. The sad man hanging on the cross no longer seemed to breathe or try to speak to him. Rudolf felt no special sorrow for that form. He had seen worse and knew that no man on the earth escaped that fate.

> *Praise the Lord, you that are his servants, praise the name of the Lord together. Blessed be the Lord's name at all times, from this day to all eternity; from the sun's rise to the sun's setting let the Lord's name be praised continually. The Lord is sovereign King of all the nations; his glory is high above the heavens. Who is like the Lord our God, so high above us, that stoops to regard both heaven and earth, lifting up the poor from the dust he lay in, raising the beggar out of his dung-hill, to find him a place among the princes, the princes that rule over his people? He gives the barren woman a home to dwell in, a mother rejoicing in her children.*

He felt instead God's compassionate urging, the same that had driven Youhanna, in spite of his own desires, his own vows of silence and poverty, and what he had long believed to be God's will, to clamber down the slope to help a stranger, a boy lying spread-eagle in the stream.

After Vespers Rudolf joined the brothers in the refectory for porridge, bread, honey and milk. They ate in silence while one brother read from the Psalms.

> *Praise ye the Lord. Blessed is the man that feareth the Lord, that delighteth greatly in his commandments. His seed shall be mighty upon earth: the generation of the upright shall be*

blessed. Wealth and riches shall be in his house: and his righteousness endureth forever. Unto the upright there ariseth light in the darkness: he is gracious, and full of compassion, and righteous. A good man sheweth favour, and lendeth: he will guide his affairs with discretion. Surely he shall not be moved forever: the righteous shall be in everlasting remembrance. He shall not be afraid of evil tidings: his heart is fixed, trusting in the Lord. His heart is established, he shall not be afraid.

Listening absently, Rudolf thought of Youhanna, seeing how the Scripture gave them all of them, though so far apart, a shared experience. Still, sooner or later, a man's own life became the book he had to read. Rudolf decided that in the morning he would seek his parents and face Gretchen. Beyond that, he could not know.

Chapter 21, Family

*Therefore do not ye be busy into the morrow, for
the morrow shall be busy to itself; for it sufficeth to
the day his own malice.* Matt. 6:34 *Wycliffe Bible*

Rudolf's last visit to Castle Schneebeli had been under circumstances so different that they seemed part of another man's life. He had ridden with his father, heavy-hearted under his father's disapproval and his own awareness of the pain he would inflict upon an innocent heart that loved him. His mother's anger beat a low drum in the background of his mind, registered in images of pursed lips and clenched fists, tight by her side. They had been a small but noble retinue on horseback, attended by his father's page. Now he was but a monk-clothed wanderer on foot, accompanied by Father Markus who would soften the shock of Rudolf's arrival by entering first and giving the news while Rudolf waited outside.

"Please tell Sir Adelbert that Father Markus is here and would like to speak to him alone, outside, immediately if he is home. If he is not, tell me when I can return and be sure of finding him."

"He is in his orchards, Father Markus. You can find him there." The servant gestured toward the hillside below the cliff against which the castle was built. "You passed him on your way here and did not see him?"

"Very likely," said Father Markus. "Our thoughts were elsewhere. Is your lady at home?" Only then did the servant notice that Father Markus was not alone. He looked curiously at the tall form in monk's habit. Father Markus watched his eyes.

"She is here."

Father Markus hesitated for a moment. Should he reveal his secret to Lady Adelbert or to his lordship?

"Should I get her for you, Father?" He believed he'd seen this other monk before, but where?

"No, no. It is all right. We will go find Sir Adelbert. God keep you." He crossed himself in blessing and turned back to Rudolf.

"All right, young lord?"

"Yes. I'm all right."

Having spotted Schneebeli's white hair in the orchard below, they took the hill in long strides. His mother's words to him when he quarreled with Conrad rang in Rudolf's ears. "Soonest ended, soonest mended."

"Your Lordship!" called Father Markus as they were near enough that Sir Adelbert could hear them.

"Father Markus! Wait a moment, I'll come to you so you don't have to walk between the trees." Sir Adelbert's concern was that the new fruit could be brushed off by the awkward priest.

Rudolf's heart pounded.

"It can't be," were Sir Adelbert's first words, having recognized Rudolf immediately. "And now you are a priest?"

"It is a long story, my lord."

"I do not doubt it. So you have brought back Rudolf, Father?"

"Not I. He returned on his own."

"Ah. Well, young man, your father's castle was destroyed by bandits who surely knew there was no one to defend it. But Heinrich is a brother to me, and he has a home here as long as he lives. Anna, too. You need not have returned on their account, Rudolf."

"I did not return on their account, my lord. I knew nothing of this until I found the castle burned."

"Why did you not come here?"

"I am here now."

"That is so. And what do you plan to do?"

"In truth, I don't know."

Sir Adelbert wanted to appear angry, but Rudolf's honesty was disarming. This young man had once known so certainly what he must do and why he must do it. The casualties of heart that fell behind had seemed to give him no pause or doubt.

"Gretchen cares for your mad and miserable mother with patience beyond any human expectation, and she does this on your behalf, for the love she has always born you. Whatever you're here for, I will not have you hurt her again."

"I do not deserve that love. No one knows that better than I. All I can say is that when I left, I was tortured by horrible fears for my own soul. I cannot explain it to you and it no longer makes much sense to me, but at the time I wanted only to die in battle because I could not take my own life."

"Take your own life? Bah! Why? You had the love of your parents and my daughter. You would be lord of this land when I am gone. Was that so bad?" Sir Adelbert gestured over the hills and the cultivated lands leading to the edge of the village of Apple Tree. His land bordered the farmland and grange of the Engelberg Abbey, an expanse of cultivation and peace below his fortress castle.

"Of course not, my lord. I could not believe that God wanted such a fate for a person as corrupt inside as I. I feared my own good fortune, Gretchen's love, that it was Satan tempting me away from God."

"I suppose the Black Robes supported that insane idea," said Sir Adelbert. "They would have everyone choose misery."

Rudolf nodded. "They confirmed my fears. I saw that going to fight for the Holy Cross would save me. My father said I would probably be killed. He said that to discourage me, but I saw only that such a death would send me straight to God. And if I were not killed? I would remain in the Holy Land until I was killed. It was simple. The vows I took seemed to answer everything."

"Seemed. It was not so simple, then?"

"No."

"What of your soul, now?"

"It is in God's keeping."

"You want to see your parents."

"Yes, my lord, even if they greet me with the anger I deserve for leaving them."

"They believe you dead."

"My mother believed my father dead until the very day he returned."

"Ah. Will you stay, Father Markus? I will take the young man back to see his parents."

"Yes," nodded the priest. He sensed the danger to Anna of Rudolf's return in her fragile condition.

"Wait here," he said to Father Markus and Rudolf, leaving them in the castle courtyard. When Sir Adelbert returned, Heinrich was leaning on his right arm and Gretchen on his left. She was no longer a childish romantic girl but a young woman, her sweet face changed not so much by time but by experience.

"Father," Rudolf said quietly, taking his father's hand.

"My boy. You are home." Tears filled the sightless eyes. He let go of Sir Adelbert and wrapped his arms around his son. Rudolf had not expected the rush of joy he felt in holding his father in his arms. All his childhood waiting for this man to return, and now this man had waited for him. It seemed their lives had been but paired longings met now in a new middle.

All of Rudolf's loss fell from him. He knew that if he told his father everything, his father would know exactly how it had been. He had taken the same journey and returned to contend with all that fate had designed for him.

"You have seen the castle?"

"Yes, father. My first night back I spent against a courtyard wall. I did not know where to go, and the fog gathered quickly. I was so tired."

"I can see that, son. Yes. What will you do with it? With Conrad gone, it is yours."

"Ours, father."

"I am no use to it now, Rudolf. I cannot see."

"I don't know yet, father."

"Here is Gretchen," he said. "This poor girl has had all she can handle in your mother and for some reason she has waited for you." Heinrich smiled. He knew how well Gretchen loved Rudolf. She blushed in embarrassment, not modesty. Rudolf let go of his father and bowed low before the girl to whom he had been betrothed.

"I rejoice to see you again, well and safe in these strange times." The words came from his deep heart. In a gentlemanly way he had said, "Thank God that you are not dead."

"Rudolf," she whispered. She crossed herself thanking God. "Please stand up so I can look at you, see it is really you."

Rudolf stood, finding it difficult to meet her eyes.

"Did you learn what you hoped to learn?" she asked, softly.

Rudolf nodded, his mouth dry, his throat choked with a tight ball of emotions he had not known he felt. Looking at Gretchen, his eyes filled with tears. Where there had been simple prettiness, Rudolf now saw the beauty that comes from strength. The song that sent him questioning?

Alas, how the sweet things poison us

I see the bitter gall floating in the honey

The white green red world is beautiful outside,

And inside black, as dark as death.

He no longer saw the "sweet things" as poison. The "sweet things" gave man reason to live here in "The white green red world [that] is beautiful outside." Death was not a terrifying inner "blackness." It was Youhanna's slumbering snow-covered peaceful form on its ledge. Rudolf's sorrow was life, a sorrow born of love, not "bitter gall floating in the honey." Life was neither gall nor honey.

"Would you see your mother now?" asked Gretchen to change the subject, to create movement in the group, which seemed paralyzed in astonishment and joy.

"She may know you, and she may not. If she does, she may rejoice but just as likely she will abuse you. All that she was, she is more now," said Sir Adelbert in a matter-of-fact voice.

Rudolf nodded. His mother seemed a faraway problem, left in the wood behind Conrad's infant shadow. Life, Youhanna, had absolved him of his responsibility to look after his little brother. He had been a man, after all, able to make a man's choices. The blue eyes behind the helmet held no accusation when he thought of them;

they had become one more of fate's inscrutable designs, a memory. In the meantime others he had loved had died and in no case could he have held back fate to save their lives.

Sir Adelbert and his wife had given Anna and Heinrich apartments off the main hall, usually used for servants, but fitted up for them to make their lives easier. Brightly colored tapestries and sunlight filtered through climbing ivy kept the room from being dismal, at least on this early summer morning. Anna lay propped on pillows, her hair in long gray braids, a cap tied beneath her chin. She looked out the window at something that seemed to have captured her attention. Rudolf later knew that this was her normal position, constantly prepared for what had not yet arrived. She waited in her madness for Heinrich, for Conrad, for Rudolf himself.

"Mother," he said softly, going to her and putting her dry, small hand between his own.

She turned and looked at him. "You're back from Sir Adelbert, then? How does pretty little Gretchen?"

Rudolf looked over at Gretchen, sitting across the bed holding his mother's hand. His face was a study in confusion. Gretchen nodded very slightly. "She's well, Mother."

"When you're married and have your babies, you must bring them to us often. The sound of children running on the stones, so lovely, so lovely. It is a pity you must live with the Schneebelis, but Conrad must have this castle, not you. Where is Conrad? In the forest, Rudolf? Have you forgotten your brother again? You will be the death of me with your selfishness. I'll send the servants to find him. You can be sure that when your father returns, he'll whip you good and hard for your carelessness. Why does he leave me here to contend with your wickedness alone?"

She closed her eyes for a few moments then, frantically demanded, "Where's my Mathilde?"

Rudolf looked at Sir Adelbert. "Your sister," he whispered. "She was four when the fire..."

Rudolf nodded.

"She burned in the fire, burned up in the fire; there was nothing left but broken stones. Conrad is also dead. Well, at least I had children and you," she said to Gretchen. "You never will. Rudolf saw to that, Rudolf, Rudolf. I saw him yesterday. He came home after visiting Sir Adelbert and said he would not marry. Where's my rosary? My rosary? Oh here, here it is." She dug into the coverlet and found where she had, for the moment, let it go. Her fingers systematically ran down the course of wooden beads. "Hail Mary, Hail Mary, Hail Mary, Hail Mary, Hail Mary, Hail Mary, Hail Mary, Our Father, Hail Mary, Hail Mary, Hail Mary, Hail Mary, Our Father, Hail Mary, Hail Mary." When her fingers reached the silver symbols of Christ's suffering, the nail, the crown of thorns, she stopped and recited the entire Pater Noster.

"She will go on like this a long time now," said Gretchen. "She'll be calm for a while."

Sir Adelbert was right. His mother WAS herself, but MORE. Her madness had freed her from the facade of dutiful wife and faithful woman. He looked at her hand on the counterpane fidgeting with her rosary, trying to find faith in the spaces between them.

That is Satan, thought Rudolf. *That is what I feared for myself.*

"Come," Sir Adelbert said, taking Rudolf's elbow. "The servants have laid some refreshments in the hall for you and Father Markus."

Rudolf turned from this creature who had given him life and went into the day's life with the others.

Each day hath his own malice, he thought, that formula for faith -- and patience. "It's awful," he said, softly, to himself.

"For us, yes, but she has no idea, Rudolf," said Lady Adelbert. "Some days she gets up to be washed and dressed and walks in the garden with Gretchen and me. She seems almost herself and chats about the things around her. At first, we thought this was a good sign and she was returning to life, but now we know it isn't. Tomorrow she may know you. You may sit and talk with her and you will feel your mother's presence again, and the next day? She will have retreated to her mind's half-light. Her days are spent reliving sad stories and building her anger. There is a battle in her soul. For all that Father Markus tries to help her, but..."

Rudolf knew there would be no Youhanna to rescue his mother from the abyss of her despair. There was no open wound to dress, no morning light in which to greet the return of the Lord. There was no sword for her to shove into the sand revealing the illusion that was her enemy. Nothing. Rudolf saw hopelessness as a plague, the perverse refuge of the cowardly.

"We must pray for her soul," sighed Father Markus. "That is our medicine. If God wills, she will defeat the enemy grasping at her heart."

Liberated by madness, nothing restrained her from the dark superstition that was her faith. Rudolf shuddered, but having seen light, he was no longer so easily fooled.

***

Returning to the monastery with Father Markus, one impression after another filled Rudolf's mind, with the painful realization that by leaving he had left his family unprotected. He and Conrad should have listened to their father and remained at home. Their family's allies were expanding their hold on all this region and the line of their castles -- fortifications and havens -- held a territory and a trade route up from the Gottard Pass across from Lake Luzern to Zürich. Heinrich's family and allies were eager to bridge the breach, but no such bridge would be built peaceably, so there were skirmishes and raids against long entrenched but now fragmented forces of the late Emperor.

Rudolf shrugged. *Each day hath his own malice*. He had returned and what would be done would be done now and in the days to come. He was not yet sure what it would be.

Chapter 22, The Morrow

When, then, we ask why a crime was done, we believe it not...A man hath murdered another; why? he loved his wife or his estate; or would rob for his own livelihood; or feared to lose some such things by him; or wronged, was on fire to be revenged. (St. Augustine, *Confessions*, Book 2)

Morning brought Sir Adelbert on horseback, ponying a horse for Rudolf. "As I recall, Conrad was the horseman, still I thought we'd look at your father's place."

Ah, thought Rudolf, *I'm surrounded not only by ghosts of the dead, but ghosts of the living as once they were.* He lifted his monk's cassock, mounted the small riding horse and was off. "I believe I can manage, Sir Adelbert," he called behind him, finding real pleasure in riding again, suddenly -- and for the first time! -- remembering with a pang the gray warhorse Sir Adelbert had given him years earlier, worlds and worlds ago.

"I thought we would talk on the way," Sir Adelbert called out. Rudolf wheeled his horse around and cantered back. Sir Adelbert was surprised to see a wide smile across the face that had been notable for its melancholy. "Tell me about these robes, Rudolf."

"It is a long story."

"What happened out there?"

"I have told that story so many times, but," Rudolf took a deep breath, "briefly, there was a battle, a horrific battle. That does not make it exceptional. What is exceptional is that I survived without wanting to, and my brother died without caring. I looked for him and couldn't find him. I left the battlefield and walked to Jerusalem. I was wounded and cared for in a hospital of lepers outside one of Jerusalem's gates. The wall itself was rubble, but the gate stood, guarded by Baibar's men, but..."

"Then?"

"I left following a caravan of refugees heading for Acre or wherever they could catch a ship out of there. I planned to reach Starkenberg and the Brotherhood, but I fell on the road unconscious and was left behind. Rightfully; what could they do? I could not walk, as my wound was infected. When I came to again, I just kept going. I fell face down in a stream in the Qaddisha Valley. A hermit, Youhanna, a Maronite, a very old man, found me and carried me up to his cave and tended my wounds. He saved not only my life but my soul."

"You are a monk, then."

"I've taken those vows, yes, Sir Adelbert." He looked at his white Cistercian robes. "But my journey home and what I've found here has turned my mind inside out."

They reached the castle ruins. In the daylight, and in the company of Sir Adelbert, Rudolf was able to make a clearer appraisal of the damage.

"Well, they were serious, whoever they were, whatever they were after."

"After the horses, yes, but perhaps they hoped for some other riches, though God knows," he crossed himself, "your father had no great treasure hidden under the paving stones. His wealth was in his horses."

Rudolf nodded. His family was in fief to von Schnabelberg. The arrangement was one of mutual help. The small castle on its promontory was one of a chain that ran across this ridge above the Reuss. Sir Adelbert's was the lowest, above this were three more. Heinrich's and the castles of Heinrich's brothers, then von Schnabelberg's with its view in all directions.

"What happened after?"

"After?"

"After you were found by the hermit."

"I wanted to die, Sir Adelbert. You know something of the things I feared that led me away from here."

"Know, yes. Understand, no. Here was a beautiful girl who loved you, a future and a home. Senseless."

Rudolf shook his head. "I will not try to explain it. I know now that a man's life has untold turnings and makes no sense to anyone but himself. Maybe not even to himself."

"That is so, young man. I cannot dispute that. Your father and I knew the same in our time, but those were different days."

"I suspect they are always different days. My life now seems to me to have been several lives and now I have returned to a place I left hoping never to see again."

"You hated it so much?"

"Not I. Conrad, yes, but not I. I feared because I loved it so. I feared my love for Gretchen, my love for the beauty of these hillsides, all of it. What if this were nothing more than the tempter trying to steal my heart from God? What if all this," Rudolf gestured, "was just a diversion?"

"Dear lord," said Sir Adelbert, crossing himself. "You take your mother's superstitions too much to heart."

"That is true, Sir Adelbert. That is precisely what I did."

"Surely your father had something to say."

"My father tried very hard to dissuade both of us. Conrad, well, I think my father knew there was no hope. Conrad's motives made sense to him. He could understand pure restlessness, but no, I think I was simply confusing."

"But you are back. That is what counts. Or maybe not. Well, certainly for your father it is everything."

"My poor father."

"You might well say that."

Rudolf knew he had been chided. It was fair, and he kept his peace. The years he'd spent as Sir Adelbert's page had taught him something about this man, his calm, his humor and sense of justice.

"And what are you prepared to do now for your poor father?"

"I'm trying to work that out. I have been back only three days and in this time I have seen my home in ruins, my mother mad and my father blind. The girl I loved is now a woman who has undertaken the care of my ranting, feeble mother. You and Lady Adelbert are, in my mind, saints, but I know you love my father and he has long been your friend. What should I do now? I've taken vows and I cannot pretend they are not important. Before those were other vows. Were they not important?"

"Only you know that, Rudolf." Sir Adelbert crossed himself, fervently praying that Rudolf would choose the path that led to Gretchen and rebuilding his father's castle, but still he knew that if Rudolf did not choose that path, they were family now.

They rode silently, single file through the forest, each lost in thoughts he could not share.

In the bright light of midmorning the castle seemed less tragic in its ruin and more a broken jug waiting for the pot healer to make his rounds. The two men dismounted and left the horses to graze on the now tall grass beside where the stables had been.

"No one had horses like Lunkhofen's horses. Remember that black? I've often wondered if things would have been different if von Schnabelberg had bought him."

Rudolf had not thought of that, but what if Conrad had not had that horse? How linked was that grand animal to Conrad's grand dreams?

"That's a good question. They were one creature."

The tower was fallen in, but not fallen down. The paving in the courtyard was in very good shape, as was one of the walls. The stones that had been the castle seemed to lie in wait.

"The tower could be repaired by the end of summer," said Sir Adelbert, maybe to Rudolf, maybe thinking aloud.

Rudolf walked in a circle beneath the open tower as startled pigeons took wing. He was remembering Gretchen here, helping his mother organize the servants for a family dinner to which his uncles had been invited as well as the Schneebelis and von Schanbelberg and his lady. His engagement to Gretchen had been announced. It had been a sweet and happy day. The courtyard had been swept clear of winter debris and all around were the beginning buds of spring. A few late crocuses bloomed among the narcissus on the hillside, pussy willow and whippletrees at the edge of the forest and along the stable walls. Conrad had been working his colt that morning and Rudolf could imagine him as he had been then, a boy fast becoming a man, a beard pushing through the child's complexion, in heart and soul the same age as the shining 4-year-old colt. Conrad had been one more shining colt of Heinrich's stable, goodhearted, generous, fierce and filled with joy, loping and bucking against the confines of his world. Rudolf's heart cleft in longing and in sorrow, and when Sir Adelbert came to join him, Rudolf's tear-streamed face turned to welcome him.

Without a word, the older man wrapped his arms around the younger man. "We can talk all day about what happened. No doubt there were times you felt yourself to blame, but," Sir Adelbert hesitated, "there was no one who could have stopped him. He went into his fate filled with joy. No doubt he died so."

Rudolf had not thought of that, that the glory and valor and honor of combat, though it led to death, would have enraptured Conrad and his wild yearning for the world. Just that first moment, with the whirling dust, the red streamers of the Khwaresmian forces, the sounds of the pipe and drums, the call, "*Gott mit Uns!*" would have thrilled Conrad's very soul. Where others would have been afraid, Conrad would only have felt, "For this moment I was born."

"What would your brother have done had he come back? A wild one, he. Would there have been a world wide enough for him?"

Rudolf shook his head. "I had not thought of Conrad in that way, Sir Adelbert."

"No. What I know of you? You probably thought you killed him with your own hand."

Rudolf nodded.

"That's your mother speaking. She could not...well, no matter. I will not speak ill of your mother to you, but she blamed you always for things you could not have changed."

Rudolf shrugged. He had not known that others saw this. "What's past is past. She is the only mother I will ever have, good or ill."

"True enough, my boy, true enough."

The two men walked down to the ruined stables. Rudolf kicked burned and broken boards out of the way. The back wall still stood.

"They did not waste much time," said Sir Adelbert, looking around. "Set the fire, took the horses and ran."

"Looks like it," agreed Rudolf. "I think they were real horse thieves."

Sir Adelbert nodded. "Your father always says so."

"How was he hurt?"

"A blow to the head. He was coming from the stables. He and his groom had bedded down the horses. He says he was hit from behind. The groom was killed. Beyond that, he doesn't know. When he came to, his sight was blurry, but he could see the castle was on fire and ran as well as he could to save your mother and the little girl, Mathilde. You know their rooms were in the top of the tower there. He got your mother, but the roof collapsed before he could reach your sister and her nurse. He brought Anna to us that night. We took them in. Your father was sure his vision would clear in time, but little by little he lost it. That was God's gift." Sir Adelbert crossed himself. "If your father had gone blind instantly, it would have broken him."

If Heinrich were not broken now, what was he? Rudolf would have to learn.

"I must go back, Rudolf. They will wait dinner for me. Will you come back with me?"

Rudolf hesitated, unsure of his duty at this moment. His parents had lived with the Schneebelis for two years. He had been home three days. He wished he could just take off over the hills with Sir Adelbert's horse or better even, to walk for days in solitude making sense of everything. Rudolf understood Youhanna's hermit yearnings well; they were natural, also, to him. "Sir Adelbert, I..."

"You need to think."

"Yes."

"You have taken monastic vows and you are afraid."

"It is not only that. I have learned something about myself. I have never been Conrad. It's never been my way to plunge forward, and when I did..."

"Ah. That is true, Rudolf. You were always a thoughtful one, even as a boy. I'll leave you then. You'll come to us tomorrow?"

"I don't know. I need to pray and to listen to God and to put everything together. I want to do what's right. I don't want to make more mistakes."

"As you wish, Rudolf. Don't wait too long."

"No."

"Keep the horse for now. You may want her."

"Thank you."

Sir Adelbert rode swiftly down the slope toward the wide green hill below which the village nestled safely in the sunlight, rimmed by apple trees. Rudolf turned the other way and, putting up the dun mare, went to his cell to pray.

Rudolf followed the monastic rules of prayer, study, work and hours of silence. No one came to interrupt his gentle quest. Even Father Markus made no attempt to penetrate Rudolf's retreat. He remembered well the strange confession made by this young man just a few years earlier. He had not understood it then and was sure there was much to Rudolf that was beyond his comprehension. Even he, a priest, had never felt such deep concern over sin, not his, not those of others. Blessed St. Bernard had laid things out clearly for all to see and understand, or so it had always seemed to him. The Black Robes were a different story, but they had not returned. With the death of the Emperor and the French King's failed Crusade, the attention of the Pope was on heretics, not infidels, and so turned the attention of the Black Robes. The Pope sent the Teutonic Knights to deal with the pagan Rus. As far as Father Markus knew all a man needed for a peaceful soul was faith in God, honest labor, regular hours, a life of charity and the brotherhood of like-minded men. Wife and family were for those God had so designed. "Ah," he thought, "that will be the young lord's question."

Father Markus had found the heart of Rudolf's dilemma without ever speaking to Rudolf. What solution was there for Rudolf's ruined family but to rebuild it, and who was there to do that work but Rudolf? Would he turn from the service of God to the service of man? Would he see in the service of man the service of God? Such it was in Father Markus' eyes. He was certain Rudolf had never set out to become a monk, or even a warrior. He had set out only to be killed. Father Markus crossed himself at that unholy

209

thought, though he knew it to be true -- as doubtless God knew as well. That failing him, Rudolf had become a monk. Father Markus suspected that Rudolf would be driven by his duty and seek a way to reconcile his duty to God and his duty to his family.

"Holy Father," prayed Father Markus, "please do not let him take too long."

Chapter 23, Anna

My son, forget not my law; but let thine heart keep my commandments: For length of days, and long life, and peace, shall they add to thee. Let not mercy and truth forsake thee: bind them about thy neck; write them upon the table of thine heart: So shalt thou find favour and good understanding in the sight of God and man. Trust in the Lord with all thine heart; and lean not unto thine own understanding. In all thy ways acknowledge him, and he shall direct thy paths.
Proverbs 3:1-6

Rudolf first looked to his friend St. Augustine for help with his dilemma, but on every page St. Augustine argued for turning away from the world of men and toward the world of God. Rudolf prayed and fasted and read, suspended again in the question of his soul's safety. Would he, as Augustine wrote, surrender his soul to Satan by returning to his family? When Rudolf realized that he looked to St. Augustine for reasons to return to his mother and father, to rebuild the castle, he knew what he must do. But how?

The answer came on a cold and rainy June morning. A messenger from the Schneebeli castle came for him. Father Markus hurried down the corridor to Rudolf's cell. "You must go, young lord. Your mother is dying."

Rudolf's heart leapt and he shrank from himself in horror at his feeling. He wanted her to die? No. He had simply wanted an answer to his question and now it had come. It could have come another way, but fate had chosen this. "Sir Adelbert's horse is being readied. You can ride down with the messenger. I'll go with you."

Rudolf nodded and put his newly cleaned cloak over his cassock to protect him from the wet and cold, and so when he and Father Markus arrived at the Schneebeli castle, Rudolf looked something like the boy who had ridden away so long ago.

Lady Adelbert met him at the gate. "Peace to you, Lady, and to your family at this time." Father Markus had come prepared. Anna's hope lay in dying in a state of grace.

"She's having problems breathing. She's in between worlds right now. She needs you, Father."

"Wait here, young lord, and you, Lady Adelbert, stay with him." Father Markus went to Anna's room and sent Heinrich, Sir Adelbert and Gretchen outside to wait.

He found Anna struggling for air. Her hair, wet with sweat, lay spread on her pillow, framing her pale, laboring face with its blue lips and pinched nostrils.

"Daughter," said Father Markus, placing the crucifix of Anna's rosary in her hand. Her fingers closed round it by habit or by reflex. He set the Body of Christ in a silver dish next to Anna's bed before sprinkling holy water throughout her room, repeating, "Hear us, holy Lord, almighty Father, eternal God: and be pleased to send Thy holy angel from Heaven to guard, cherish, protect, visit and defend all that dwell in this house. Through Christ our Lord."

"Lady Lunkhofen, your life has been, as are all our lives on earth, filled with sorrow. I know you have yearned for God but often He has eluded you. Can you confess your sins to me now?" The priest sighed. He had hoped she would be able to relieve herself of her anger and superstition in the final moments of her earthly life. Miracles were known to happen just before the body's openings were blessed with the holy oil. It was a rite not meant only to ease the passing of the soul into the next world, but to heal the body for further efforts in this one. He decided to sit down for a moment and wait in prayer. Perhaps Anna would feel the presence of God and open her eyes, but her breath remained ragged and labored, and her eyes didn't open. She didn't seem to know that Father Markus was in the room. He began to fear that if he waited longer, it would be too late for Anna's one hope of Heaven.

In the shape of a cross, he placed the holy oil on Anna's lips, eyes, ears, nose, hands and feet, absolving her of all sins she had committed through the openings through which the soul could be tempted. Making the sign of the cross over her body, he relieved her of any sin of the flesh she might have committed in deed or desire, saying each time, "By this holy unction and his own most gracious mercy, may the Lord pardon you whatever sin you have committed."

He placed the body of Christ between Anna's lips and called the others to the room. They entered in silence, their feelings mixed between relief and sorrow.

"Our help is in the Name of the Lord," said Father Markus. "Remember not, Lord, the offenses of Thy handmaid, and take not vengeance on her sins. Our Father . . ." began Father Markus, and the prayer was spoken together.

"O Lord, hear my prayer."

"And let my cry come to Thee."

"The Lord be with you."

"And with thy spirit."

"Let us pray," said Father Markus, nearing the end, the final plea for Anna's troubled soul. "Most gracious God, Father of mercies and God of all consolation, You wish none to perish that believes and hopes in You, according to Your many mercies look down favorably upon Your handmaid, Anna, whom true faith and Christian hope commend to You. Visit her in Your saving mercy, and by the passion and death of Your only begotten Son, graciously grant to her forgiveness and pardon of all her sins that her soul in the hour of its leaving the earth may find You as a Judge appeased, and being washed from all stain in the Blood of Your same Son may deserve to pass to everlasting life. Through the same Christ our Lord."

"Amen."

"Amen."

"Now we wait," said Heinrich, sitting in his accustomed chair beside the bed of his wife. What misery he had brought upon her and she upon him! And, when it seemed she had surrendered to the past and the absence of her sons, and they began to make a new life, their daughter was lost and the castle burned. Heinrich shook his head. The wanderings of his life had taken him many places, to sights unbearable in their horror to others lovely in their wonderment. He had no regrets about his life anymore. The inability to see had turned his lively vision inward, upon his heart, to meditate the choices of his life. It now seemed to him that the times in which he lived made a man the person he was. All that turned on the wheel of fate. That his parents were married and their union led to him, that his uncles and his father were allied to a family in war against the Emperor, that a mountain pass was built making it easier to trade with the Lombards and Venetians, and that, in its turn, had led his family to this ridge above this river. Who designed that? God's will? Or simple fate? It was no different for his sons.

Rudolf stood beside his father, his hand upon the older man's shoulder. "I'm happy you have returned, my son," said Heinrich, softly, reaching his hand to place it over his son's. "It has been lonely here without my boys or even hope of your return. Perhaps someday you'll tell me all that happened, though I can imagine..."

"I will, Father."

Anna never loosed her grip on the rosary and in that Father Markus, at least, took hope. "She will be with our Lord and Savior soon, Sir Heinrich. She will find peace there, poor woman." The family stayed around her through the long afternoon. By sunset Anna had gone. Her body was washed and wrapped. She would be buried in the monastery graveyard with the remains of her little girl.

***

"I could not make her happy, son," said Heinrich, leaning on Rudolf as they walked back to the Schneebelis, "no matter what I did."

"It was not your fault. I don't think she was born for happiness."

"You may be right. But..." he paused. "I will not speak ill of her. No one can completely understand another person." Heinrich sighed, "I do wish I could go home to my horses."

Rudolf looked at his father. He was in the prime of life. His family was long-lived and he might yet live many years more, but living in another man's home. This must have been what Sir Adelbert had meant when he had said Heinrich was not broken. Blind, but still very much in life.

"Was anything left, father, any of your fortune or of Mother's?"

"I put most of my fortune in the horses, but some remains with my brothers who insisted I not throw it all into livestock. I suppose when they looked at me they saw something like you might have seen in Conrad."

Rudolf was surprised. "I cannot imagine that, Father."

"No, probably not." Heinrich smiled. "What will you do, Rudolf? Adelbert tells me you are a monk, that you have taken those vows."

Rudolf had forgotten his father could not see him.

"I took vows when I was with the Maronites in the Qaddisha Valley. One of them saved my life and my soul. A moment came and I joined them, but," he paused, "Khwaresmians swooped down the valley and burned everything, and I found myself on the road home."

"And Conrad? What happened, Rudolf?"

"We arrived in Acre, at the Hospice. It was almost empty. There we learned of the fall of Jerusalem, which made many of us more determined to fight. After two or three days, I don't remember exactly, we went south to a camp where what remained of our forces waited in the fierce heat for a battle to break. We trained and slept and ate and wondered when. The few survivors of the sack of Jerusalem, men from all the Orders, just wanted it to end. They waited for a door to open, a door through which they could leave that hell. The door of death or the door of victory made no difference to them any more."

Rudolf took a deep breath before he continued. Many times on his journey home he'd imagined telling all this to his father, had rehearsed it in his mind. He spoke as if from a script. "Conrad, many of us, grew impatient. We'd come to fight. We did not know how small were our forces, how small our selves. Our leaders suddenly abandoned their strategy and the battle broke like a fire. When it stopped I was alone among the dead. Conrad was killed soon after the battle started, of that I'm sure. I was with him, beside him, and then I didn't see him again. I was wounded in the thigh. I could not walk well. The dead covered the earth, even to the far horizon where the enemy had set fire to our tents. Horses and men screamed all around me. Forgive me father. I could not look for him. I continued on, hoping to die, but..."

Heinrich crossed himself. "I'm grateful you are alive, Rudolf. You cannot know how grateful." The man's sightless eyes were filled with tears. "I know what it is, the effect of that unmistakable scent of death on any living man. God designed it to make us run away from it. It is not where we belong. Son, will you, do you plan to..." Heinrich stopped.

"No, father. Our home, you, everything here is for me as I was for Youhanna. I might wish I had no duty to the world but prayer, vows and ritual, but I do."

"Youhanna?"

"The man who saved my life in Lebanon."

"Schneebeli told me some of that. A desert hermit? There are many such holy men. I recall them from my journey home. I sometimes saw their caves on high cliff walls. Perhaps I saw your Youhanna's cave. The Maronites are good farmers. Their olive groves covered the hillsides, though how they cultivated anything in that dry dirt is a mystery. Not like here."

Heinrich might have taken a drink from Youhanna's stream, looked up and seen Youhanna's cave, his olive grove.

"I spent hours with him tending his trees and listening to him. I — he had to abandon the life he desired in order to save me. When he saw my life held fast, but my soul did not, he turned his care to that, to bringing my soul into the light of life and God."

"How long were you with him?"

"Two years? When Youhanna died, I joined the brethren. I would be there still if they had not been chased out and killed. The monastery was burned to the ground. I came away with my monk's habit, Youhanna's goatskin bags, a book I transcribed myself in the monastery scriptorium, and a Khwaresmian knife I found in the dirt. On the way, in Modona, I was given this cloak by another knight, Sir Götz."

"Modona. Yes. The intersection of the world. And Venice?"

"Yes. On the way out and back it seemed like two different cities. On the way, it seemed to me a city of mystery, beauty and sin. I worried so much about Conrad, but... Returning? A misty way-station of secrets. I stayed with the Brotherhood for a few days, then many of us left Venice. Our ways diverged where they went east. When I reached the Po, I turned my cloak inside out and came home."

"Alive." Heinrich clasped the young man tightly in his arms. "Oh, my son. I thank God."

***

A meal had been laid under the trees in the Schneebeli orchard for the funeral guests, with a table for Heinrich and the family to one side. Rudolf took his father to his place of honor at the table beside Sir Adelbert. Rudolf found he had been seated next to Gretchen. He was sure it was no accident. As he took his seat, Gretchen said, in a low voice, almost a whisper, "I'm sorry, Rudolf."

"Maybe now my mother has found the peace she was looking for. She was a terrible weight on your family."

"Your mother and father are my family too, Rudolf. You forget that."

"I have not forgotten anything." Beneath the tablecloth, Rudolf took Gretchen's hand in his.

Seeing crimson climb his daughter's pale cheeks, Sir Adelbert smiled in broad joy down the table at his wife who, smiling back, leaned to whisper in Heinrich's ear.

Heinrich smiled and waved his hand toward the dirge-strumming musician. "Minnesinger! Come over here," he called. "I have something to ask of you." The musician stopped his song and walked over to Heinrich under the apple tree and tapped his shoulder.

"My lord?"

"Would you play something else? We have had sorrow enough. Mourning and sadness will not change anything or bring back one day. Play a song. Do you know," he hummed a melody.

"I do, sir. Are you sure?"

"I am sure."

The musician returned to his partners and, after the surprised drummer hesitantly struck an upbeat, much faster rhythm, the singer, who had never heard of such a song at a funeral banquet, lifted his mandolin and, knowing he would soon shock everyone, began,

The powerful winter has left us behind,
and lovely is the summertime;

now I eye the woods and moors,
leaves and flowers, and a pretty clover
thence I want our joy never to melt away.

Afterward

A Note about Minnesangs

Popular music, played by troubadours, was part of courtly life in the thirteenth century. In the German speaking world this kind of music was called "Minnesangs" because they were (supposedly) about trivial subjects, in other words, not religious songs.

Possibly the most famous Minnesang is Walther von der Vogelweid's "Under the Linden" in which the subject is the warm glow after love making. The speaker — a woman — speaks of how the grass has been bent under them and her lips are red and sore from their kissing.

> *Under the linden tree*
> *on the open field,*
> *where we had our bed,*
> *you can still see*
> *lovely broken flowers and grass.*

She goes on to say that anyone passing and looking at the spot would know immediately what happened there and would laugh about it.

Other Minnesangs were more serious. Some contained grievances against the Pope for taking so much money from the northern (German) people for crusades. Some of the Minnesangs were meant — and used — to influence people as Conrad and Rudolf are influenced by Walther von der Vogelweid's "Palästinalied." An Italian song of love and longing by Rinaldo d'Aquino speaks to Anna in Heinrich's absence.

It's for this reason I've included a few Minnesangs in this novel as ambient and important parts of the world in which Rudolf and his family lived.

Made in United States
Orlando, FL
16 March 2022

15836814R00133